Samuel Lowrie Robertson

Dora

On the Border and other Poems

Samuel Lowrie Robertson

Dora
On the Border and other Poems

ISBN/EAN: 9783337341732

Printed in Europe, USA, Canada, Australia, Japan

Cover: Foto ©Andreas Hilbeck / pixelio.de

More available books at **www.hansebooks.com**

SAMUEL L. ROBERTSON.

DORA

OR

ON THE BORDER

AND OTHER POEMS

BY

SAMUEL LOWRIE ROBERTSON

BIRMINGHAM:
ROBERTS & SON
1894

CONTENTS.

—

INTRODUCTORY POEM.

Go forth, my little untried bark,
　　I waft thee o'er a stormy sea,
And pray, that both through light and dark,
Some kindly eyes thy course shall mark;
　　And placid waves shall roll for thee,
　　And winds propitious be.

Yet stronger, nobler barks, perchance,
　　Than thou art, have been shaken sore,
What time they passed some Magi's haunts,
Whose wand forbade them to advance,
　　Or led them to some treacherous shore,
　　Whence sailed they nevermore.

But by their fate be not dismayed,
　　They may have suffered of their weight:
Had they been shallops, light arrayed,
They might have o'er the wild waves played,
　　And 'scaping from the storms, elate,
　　Have known a happier fate.

So take thy fortune with the rest;
   Thy sails for rudest buffets trim ;
Thus of thy worth is made the test :
Whatever is to be, is best
   For each fame-seeker—her or him—
   Whose motto's 'sink or swim.'

If such thy hardy motto be,
   And duteous thou dost venture make,
Then triumph or defeat, for thee
Shall prove a moral victory ;
   And patient praise or blame thou'lt take,
   As I will for thy sake.

DORA

OR

ON THE BORDER

A soldier of the mountain land,
Of shoulder broad and brawny hand,
Albeit a hundred slaves had he,
With them he felled and split the tree,
Oft ploughed the furrow, plied the hoe,
And 'twas his pride to lead the row;
He ne'ertheless, their master, knew
The labor each and all should do.
Yet during happy holidays—
And these were many—in their plays,
Their songs and dances, oft would he
Participate with equal glee.
And through the mountains many a night,
With horn and hound in wild delight,
With Judah, Zekel, Pomp, and Clay,

—2

Would chase the fox till break of day,
The sly "ole possum "—"ole Zip coon "
Pursue and catch beneath the moon,
And weary, broken down at last,
Joined them in their own rude repast
Of bacon broiled and ash cake sweet—
Delicious bread—delicious meat.

*   *   *   *   *   *   *   *

This soldier of the mountain land
Of shoulder broad and brawny hand,
But little book lore had, and yet
His thought tow'rds fairyland was set,
And much sang he, and many a time
With unpremeditated rhyme,
Though rude indeed, he builded lays
In many a rustic maiden's praise.
But one, far lovelier than the rest,
At first, but an invited guest
Within the portals of his heart,
Took lodgment and would not depart;
And o'er the landscape of his thought,
So hot, so quick, so vig'rous--brought
The hazy pensiveness of love.

She—in his heart preferred above
His own chief good—demanded still
His dreams, as uttered by his quill.
And so, while lone he paced his round
A charm in song to her he found,
When, spite of rain, or sleet, or snow,
Thus poured he forth his joy and woe:

I.

The river rolling by thy door,
　The far off hills among,
Here at its mouth—its journey o'er
　Brings me, methinks, thy song;
　　And not in sorrow but delight
　　I stand a sentry here tonight.

II.

Though dark and deep the river's flow,
　Beneath this happy moon,
It has a murmur soft and low,
　Almost to me a tune,
　　Like the echoes of thy sweet guitar,
　　To me soft floating from afar.

III.

A fond sweet fancy is this? nay,
　No voice of music dies :

Some bird of air—some woodland fay—
  Some angel sweet and wise,
    Preserves this breath of heaven for men,
    Who snatch it from their shells again.

IV.

Ah, if 'twere mine, on such a night
  As this, thy hand to press,
With rapture's unrestrained delight,
  And Love's fond tenderness,
    My spirit would itself resign,
    To cruel fate and not repine.

V.

There comes a soft voice from the hills,
  Like that from stormless seas,
And its sweet breathing gently thrills
  The wind harps of the trees ;
    All that it needs to be divine
    Is to be mingled, love, with thine.

VI.

The stars outpour their softest beams,
  Like gentle, lovelit eyes ;
The night winds loll upon the streams,
  And cloudless are the skies :
    One thing is wanting to beguile
    My sadness, darling--thy dear smile.

VII.

Tomorrow morn these waters clear
  May roll ensanguined by,
For the roaring, night and day, I hear,
  Like the blue vaults thund'rous sigh,
    Of far off guns from o'er the hills,
    And my soul with solemn awe it fills.

VIII.

Good-bye—even now the opening gun
  To battle calls— I go
To take my fate in Donelson,
  Beleaguered by the foe.
    The Blue and Grey are mustering fast—
    The death work is begun at last.

IX.

Good-bye, good-bye!   Ah, if you knew—
  Ha ! I must drop my pen ;
Too thick the bullets whistle through
  The camp—good-bye again ;
    Now may propitious stars be mine,
    And none but sweet ones o'er you shine.

DORA'S REPLY.

"I promised to write you a letter,"
   Thus Dora, her letter began,
"But somehow I think it were better—
   You being a sensible man—
To check up a little and think,
Ere we get into trouble with ink.

"To me you are ever so pleasant
   And charming betimes, I must own,
But fancies are things evanescent,
   And dreams like the flowers are blown ;
Now I tell you most earnestly, friend,
'Twere best some of yours had an end.

"A glorious soldier I paint you ;
   Ambitious, courageous and free
From all that can blacken or taint you,
   As any poor mortal can be ;
And a hero I think you must prove
If you shake off the shackles of love

"You see I am chatting you plainly,
   And giving a lick, not a blow,
To keep you from acting insanely
   And plunging headlong into woe :
For in me one conviction obtains :
You would never work well in my chains.

"Of course I may change my opinion,
  For such you must patiently wait,
Meantime can't you fight for dominion,
  And strive like a man with your fate,
And doing your duty proclaim
Your title to honor and fame?

"When you answered her call you decided
  To give to your country your life;
A head and a heart undivided
  She'll need both, I wot, in this strife.
And heaven with them, on her side,
If safe through this tempest she ride.

"A woman, I know you would hate her,
  Who caused you our cause to desert
When it needed you most, like a traitor,
  By giving it half of your heart;
So lest you should hate me at last,
Let's try now to bury the past.

"A battle this moment is raging,
  I hear o'er the waters its roar,
The Blue and the Gray are engaging:
  Soon, soon, may these horrors be o'er;
Yet I feel—aye, I know—even now,
You are winning a crown for your brow.

"God keep you, my brave, and protect you,
    Nor shorten your life's little span,
But even in danger direct you
    To 'scape it and yet be a man ;
And yours be all merited bays
And His be the glory and praise."

*   *   *   *   *   *   *   *

" Now tell me true if, like the idle breeze
Which steals unnoticed through the leafy trees,
The sighs I give you pass without regard,
Nor for a moment joy's pursuit retard.
Are sighs of mine such foolish, trifling things
They are no more than streamlet murmurings?
Or sinking in the ear do they break through
And touch your heart?   Oh, tell me true!

" Oh, tell me true! if, like the voice of bells,
As homeward come the cows from grassy dells,
My words attention claim but for the while,
Yet have no charm fond memory to beguile.
Have words of mine no sweetness and no spell,
And in remembrance do they scarcely dwell;
Or do they smite the ear and breaking through
Possess the mind?   Oh, tell me true!

"Oh, tell me true! if, like the fading bowers
Which 'mind us Eden is no longer ours,
The light and shadow of my face but wake
The dream of joys we must no more partake.
Do they no longer touch, awake, enchant?
Or as of old, do they your spirit haunt,
And taking hold on memory still renew
Love's olden fires?   Oh, tell me true!"

Thus homeward flying on his way
From Shiloh, Ap Dahlgreen so gay,
Came singing as he neared the cot
Of her by him still unforgot—
Of Dora, loved with love so true,
For dreams or hopes he scarcely knew :
But by some trick of fancy were
Connected in some way with her.
On march or picket all the same
Some sights or sounds recalled her name,
And even in battle's smoke and din
Her best loved image came to win
A moment's pray'r—in ev'ry scene
Her mem'ry haunted Ap Dahlgreen ;
To her flowed all his thoughts and dreams,
As riverward flow all the streams.

*   *   *   *   *   *   *   *

And strange as if some bird of air
Was whisp'ring her his spirit's prayer;
She, too, at twilight's pensive time
Delights to weave and sing her rhyme,
Blushing to hear her own guitar
In tinklings—tell it to her star:

"Oh, gallant friend! in dreams of Auld Lang Syne,
'Twas bliss to find you kneeling at my shrine;
But now, alas! I look into the core
And see you knocking vainly at the door;
Yet should you turn away and cease to plead
My heart would beat in loneliness, indeed,
For oh, I love to think—to dream—of you!
As my best friend, my friend most true.

"Oh, gallant friend! my heart is like the rose,
Not to each zephyr's kiss it beauteous blows:
One gives it beauty—glory, day by day—
Another steals its very soul away.
Thus do your smiles bring gladness to my heart,
But do not shake it—pierce it like a dart,
And disenchanted still my soul remains,
Not touched—not trammeled by your chains.'

Then to herself she softly said,
Glancing around as half afraid

To give an utterance to her thought,
Lest to his ears it might be brought :
" If I could sing these words to you
Then might you swear I loved you true."
And turning to the chords again
She sang a more impassioned strain :

SONG.

Come o'er the hills to me,
　Come with the falling dew,
Waiting am I for thee,
　My love, my dear, so true.
Come with thy lambent eyes
　Melting with fires repressed,
And let them forth in sighs —
　· I'll know. my love, the rest.

Come, when the morning star
　Heralds the rosy dawn,
Come with the golden car
　That brings the day god on.
Give me thy witching smile,
　Sweeter than theirs its shine ;
Never can they beguile
　The night as it does mine.

Come 'neath the blazing noon,
   Hot like my love for thee;
Kiss me as passionate June
   Kisses the wandering sea.
Then all the hours we'll sing,
   Morning, and noon, and night,
And grief shall plume her wing
   And from our lives take flight.

*   *   *   *   *   *   *   *

John Dacre was a moody man,
  Who had fled the city's haunts,
Where erst a stormy race he ran
  And made and lived romance.
    He with his child had sought a home
    Where none but hunters dared to come.

Sequestered there in a deep cove,
  A vine embowered retreat,
The mountains frowning from above,
  The river at his feet,
    In cottage rude he spent his years,
    And hid from man his sighs and tears.

Ere long it was to him a shrine—
  A kind of holy place,
Where ev'ry bower of rose and vine
  With beauty, peace and grace
    Enwreathed it—made it Eden fair ;
    And his Dora was the goddess there.

A student in his early days,
  His books companions were,
And not unskilled in am'rous lays,
  These he sang and taught to her,
    Who, with him 'neath the evening star,
    Discoursed them on the sweet guitar.

Nor were the hunter's arts untaught :
  To shoot, to row, to ride ;
Next to the joys, which music brought,
  Her steed the most supplied ;
    Still like an oarsman skilled she knew
    Each motion of her frail canoe.

Yet not an Amazon in form,
  Nor one in heart was she,
A natural creature, strong and warm,
  From the artificial free.
    The bloom and beauty of good health
    And true development were her wealth.

She was not, as the saying goes,
    Gentle, but sweet and warm as June,
And looked a landscape in repose
    Beneath a pensive summer moon.
        But ever and anon would flash
        Gleams from the enclosure of her lash,
        When dark and trembling drooped the lid
        That showed fierce passion 'neath it hid.

Her eye was hazel when it danced
    With sweet anticipation—so
Its mirth and gladness all entranced ;
    But when it had an angry glow,
        It was a dark, clear, glittering gray,
        Which seen you could not put away—
        It thrilled you like a lightning spark,
        And left your thoughts confused and dark.

But almost perfect was her form,
    Lovely beyond the loveliest dream
Of poet, sculptor, lover ; warm,
    Voluptuous, graceful, sweet—a theme—
        A model for the fiery pen :
        Seen once, until 'twas seen again,
        You felt a sense of loss, and owned
        Your dream of beauty in her throned.

She was well-suited to the wild :
  Rocks, trees and vines her partners were,
And that dark river where the child
  Long lingered, had a charm for her.
    And when to maidenhood she grew
    She plied it in her light canoe :
    Its majesty and myst'ry strong
    Crept up into her veins ere long.

She was indeed a being strange,
  Such as a gentle man admires :
In her, no matter what his range
  Of fancy or of mad desires,
    Was that which satisfied them quite.
    Her voice, her motions, gave delight ;
    You loved and feared her, too, at length—
    Her greatest weakness was her strength.

Such was John Dacre's Paradise
  When war disturbed the land,
And threw its gloom athwart the skies
  And its bolts from strand to strand,
A most unwelcome visitor
  Next to death itself, to him and her.

He was all Southern every vein—
  Was hot with Southern blood—

The sight of blue coats fired his brain,
   Peopled his solitude
With ugly devils ; night and day
   As 'twere, upon his arms he lay.

But Dora's voice grew sweeter now—
   More glorious seemed her eyes ;
Each morn and eve he kissed her brow
   And called her sweet and wise,
And asked her if another's love,
   As strong and true as his would prove.

"This morning," thus John Dacre said,
   "This very morning, Fanny says,
A squad of bold marauders, led
   By a picked leader, comes to ' Fez,'
     What his vile purpose—aim may be—
     Is not a mystery to me.

" Twice has he passed this nest of ours—
   His weary horses watered here :
The man has dared to pluck my flowers
   And 'cross the fence at you to leer ;
     In arrogance e'en grown so fat
     He'd dare to you to doff his hat.

" He comes here now with purpose dire
   By violence to pluck a rose,

Which taken from your lordly sire
　Will harm him more than deadliest blows;
　　In very spite for scorn of mine,
　　He threats to snatch you from my shrine.

"He'd make me take the traitor's oath,
　Or go with him to prison walls,
Thus robbing me indeed.　Too loth
　Am I, e'en when my country calls,
　　To leave these precincts, sweet, and you,
　　With blood my clean hands to imbue.

"I hate bloodshed and war, but driven
　To strife for your and honor's safe,
I shall commend my soul to heaven,
　And chances on the issue take;
　　He shall not trample on my rights—
　　Heav'n still the just man's wrongs requites.

"He tells our Fanny, if again
　To me or you his hat he doff
In courtesy, and we refrain
　From recognition—but rebuff
　　Him by the faintest look of scorn—
　　We'll rue the day that we were born.

"The insolent upstart—both shall rue
　His wakened anger—let it wake;
——3

Now I will die and so shall you,
  Before one nod to him I make;
    Before I'll budge one foot, to assuage
    This bully's temper, spleen or rage.

" Nor on his passions shall we wait,
  And thus chivalric patience show,
His movements we'll anticipate
  And meet his threats with the first blow ;
    And woe to him if he should come
    In forty paces of our home."

" But, father, hear me," Dora cried,
  " A few miles off is Ap Dahlgreen "—
" Tush! Ap Dahlgreen! You have no pride,
  Your flight to him, what would it mean ?
    In peace we've lived alone thus far,
    And we can die alone in war.

" No! Coming back what would we find ? —
  Our home in ashes. Tut! you fear ;
But go you.. I will stay behind,
  And give the fellow welcome here,
    A warm reception, such as men
    Wisely decline to risk again."

" But father, hear me still, this once ;
  Fear prompts no utterance of my tongue ;

Though but a girl, I am no dunce,
  Nor am my woman's nerves unstrung
    By come or coming danger—nay.
    For valor's better part I pray.

" I love this home, but what to me
  Were Paradise itself—ay, heaven,
Parted from you? What would they be,
  If to despair my soul were driven?
    Parting from you is my chief dread,
    Father, as living or as dead.

" But hush, they come—hear how they sing,
  How boist'rous, rude they ride ! now, see,
Am I afraid? I'll clip his wing
  If he but fly in reach of me.
    One gun—one " Colt "—a fort like this,
    Ha ! ha ! I'll show him I'm no *miss*."

*   *   *   *   *   *   *   *

With ribald song and drunken shout
  The troopers galloped down the pass ;
Ay, tumbled, so to speak, a rout—
  A ruffian-like, disordered mass :
    Some, spite of drunken beastliness,
    Betraying caution ne'ertheless.

Two double-barreled guns they had,—
    The father and the daughter--two
Good "navies."   They were fiercely glad,
    As on the foe a "bead" they drew;
        Each, through a broken window pane,
        Watching the score of horse to rein.

They dashed up to the gateway.   "Halt!
    Prepare, boys, to dismount."   "Now! now!
If they escape us 'tis our fault,
    No forming into line allow.
        Down, Dora, with the huddled four."
        "Bang! bang!"—they tumbled o'er.

"Bang! bang!"—John Dacre could but yell
    To see the troopers scatter, fly;
A pistol shot—another fell—
    But danger seeming to defy
        The dauntless leader sat his steed,
        To buckshot giving little heed.

Bang! 'twas a shotgun—horse
    And rider reeled—struck—wailing both,
And many a groan and many a curse
    Was heard, of mingled pain and wrath.
        Five wounded dragged themselves away,
        But the brave leader prostrate lay.

Not one unwounded braggart stayed
  Beside his fallen comrades—each.
No fire returning, fled dismayed
  Beyond each deadly missile's reach;
    Or up the sheltering mountain's side,
    Or on his horse's speed relied.

But one, a proud, chivalric son
  Of the "dark and bloody ground,"
Bethought him that his race was run,
  So fearful was his wound—
    A young lieutenant, Cad Leflore,
    He grieving cursed his captors sore.

But Dora's heart was kind as brave,
  And she pitied him the more,
The more she saw him writhe and rave,
  His wounds and bondage o'er;
    And she began to feel a joy
    Nursing this fierce Kentucky boy.

What heart so hard—what soul so dark—
  But kindness melts apace:
But kindles to the electric spark,
  Flashed from a lovely face,
    And wakened by a gentle touch
    To extremes flies often over much?

Day after day, the Spring time past,
  He ceased to mourn his lot;
Some gladness had each hour, and fast
  Time vanished by his cot;
    For Dora, brave, and sweet, and mild,
    Both nursed him back to life, and smiled.

A stately, stalwart youth was he,
  And in his luminous eye
And haughty lip one glance could see
  Courage and purpose high;
    Milder and gentler, day by day
    His manners waxed, till he was gay.

Ah, loving kindness ! what a spell
  Stronger than Circe's own,
Seems in thy look—thy touch—to dwell,
  To all but thee unknown;
    Thou castests devils out, and mirth
    Their places takes at the madman's hearth.

If words of love between them passed,
  'Twas such as bubbled o'er
Their barriers—not to be repressed
  Or shut up in the core;
    They unpremeditated sprung
    And slipped unguarded from the tongue.

Then was each brow beclouded—each
    With half confusion spoke :
The soul and fire had left their speech
    Quick as just now it broke
        The bounds of prudence—ne’ertheless
        The palm-words they could not repress.

Though ever and anon the glance
    Of olden hate returned,
Their breasts no longer were hate’s haunts :
    Love replaced it there and burned.
        At first he shone a lurid flame,
        At last in perfect blaze he came.

Dear woman, though at first she’d hate,
    To reviling and to curses
If not to killing—soon or late
    Ends in loving, what she nurses.
        With what she pities sympathizes :
        What she hates today, tomorrow prizes.

The thought that burned in mutual eyes,
    And in fiery touch of hands,
And sent out skirmishers in sighs,
    Followed by conquering bands
        Of burning words and strong caresses :—
        The child observer knows what this is.

But the old man was not glad to see
　That "mutual" in their eyes,
"This will not do—no, no," quoth he,
　"Love is braver than he's wise;
　　I have spared—will spare this fellow's life—
　　But my daughter must not be his wife.

"A hateful, hated traitor he,
　A dastard matricide;
A Southern born—great heaven! see,
He boasts with wonted pride
　　That he has ripped his Southland up,
　　And made her drink the bitter cup.

"Dora, poor fool—I thought her wise,
　I thought her brave and strong—
Has found enchantment in his eyes
　And sweetness in his song;
　　And sighs whene'er the reptile moans,
　　And trembles when the traitor groans."

Thus raged he, pacing to and fro
　His cottage hall alone;
When slyly Dora dared to show
　These verses and make known
　　More certainly, what most he feared :—
　　What stabbed a heart already seared.

* * * * * * * *

Thou dost not know the sacred flame
   That lights my bosom's inner shrine,
Yet burns it there for thee the same—
     My heart is thine.

Thou seest the darkened brow alone,
   Not the glad Cupid's eyes that shine.
Whene'er I see thee—hear thy tone—
     My heart is thine.

Beneath my visage stern and cold
   Doth lurk a passion sweet as wine,
And love that still must be untold—
     My heart is thine.

From gloom we snatch the brightest brand,
   And potent fire from saddest shrine,
And tend'rest love from roughest hand—
     My heart is thine.

When spring is wet with od'rous dews,
   When summer's glory's in decline,
And autumn's tears her cheeks suffuse—
     My heart is thine.

When winter shakes her hoary hairs,
   Yet in her ingle burn and shine

Sweet fires, like these my bosom bears—
 My heart is thine.

Through all the changes of the days
 That give the year its shade and shine,
By all life's smooth or rugged ways—
 My heart is thine.

* * * * * * * *

Not slow to mark the cool regard
 Upon the old man's brow,
The smile of welcome gone—'twas hard
 To meet his glances now—
  Not slow to see all this and more,
  As 'twas expected—was Leflore.

Nor did love's madness and regret,
 Nor Dora's smiles and tears
So blind him, that he could forget
 The counsel of his fears,
  That he was but a captured foe:
  His captor's anger was his woe.

Though claiming now in his brave breast
 Love's superadded strength,
His courage found the sorest test

In the old man's frown at length ;
  This was an omen dark, and said
  That storms were in his pathway spread.

" Now ride, Leflore—our boys are here,"
  One morning Dora cried ;
" You know the path, my love, my dear,
  Leflore, for God's sake, ride ;
    Some one your hiding has betrayed,
    Their captain cannot be delayed.

" 'Tis Ap Dahlgreen—you know—you know ;
  See, father's by his side,
No questions ask—this instant go,
  Your horse is ready—ride."
    And scarcely from the barn he sped
    Ere bullets whistled round his head.

She wrung her hands, she laughed, she cried,
  She danced in almost glee,
As spurring up the mountain side,
  Leflore was gone—was free.
    But no! one bullet sped too true,
    The wounded horse his rider threw.

The old man saw it not, again
  He seemed to breathe with joy,

And clasped each one of Johnson's men
  Exultant as a boy.
    But Dora saw her lover's fall,
    And pursuit endeavored to forestall.

In vain, she called to Ap Dahlgreen :
  He paused not, but his men
Urged on, and swore in ugly spleen
  He would lead them ne'er again.
    Leflore, meantime, rock shelter had,
    And to pursuit defiance bade.

   *   *   *   *   *   *   *   *

Another scene—a light canoe
  Swept down the river dark and wide,
In haste a furious troop pursue
  Along a craggy mountain side,
Which overtops with bluff and slope
  The waters darkly rolling by,
And now through tarns the horsemen grope,
  And now through canebrake slow they hie.

All through the Summer day, 'neath skies
  Which looked unclouded down on earth,
Two boatmen cast their anxious eyes
  Across the river.   Half in mirth

They chatted as they swept along
   Beyond the reach of rifle shot,
She venturing oft a snatch of song,
   He listening mute his cares forgot.

Though hot the day, untired the two
   Impelled their shallop silent on—
The maiden paddling the canoe,
   He praising her for skill and brawn.
Across his lap his rifle lay,
   A deadly Whitworth long of range,
And with it fond he seemed to play,
   Anxious to get some shot exchange.

But hush! the river narrows here,
   The bluff shores at each other frown,
And o'er the waves the tramp they hear
   Of horse, the steep gorge coming down.
Clearer the voices, than the tramp
   Of hoofs, of horsemen, from above
Or from below, as through the swamp
   The burdened steeds could scarcely move.

Oft now Leflore his Whitworth raised,
   To fire upon some forward knight;
But Dora frowned, or at him gazed
   With look his purpose to affright.

She knew the horsemen, one and all:
  "Not now," she pleading, softly said,
"We'll reach the field ere evening's fall,
  And then we may be well afraid.

"I know them well, by day and night,
  Unstaying and unstayed they ride,
Danger to them has a delight,
  And seeking danger is their pride;
Each horseman there commands his slaves—
  A birthright claims—has acres broad,
And each a flag defiant waves
  And suppliant bows to none but God.

I would not have them kill you: No!
  I'd die to have you 'scape their wrath;
But one among them loves me so,
  Is now a sleuthhound on your path;
And if he catch you, look to die—
  I scarce could 'scape his jealous ire.
Be patient, then, the night is nigh,
  Not long we'll be in danger dire."

Perforce, because of shallows, they,
  To shun engulfing rocks and snags,
The potent current must obey,
  That swept them tow'rds the opposing crags,

Where stood the foe, with rifle true ;
   But twilight now had fallen ; " There
In that deep nook," quoth she, "may you
   Lie hid ; beyond, the banks are bare."

They touch the bank—" Hush ! who comes there ? "
   Comes from a deep and sheltered cove.
" Friend," cried Leflore, in half despair,
   " Halt there and do not further move."
" Come in ! come in ! " another cries ;
   " Surrender ! " cries another.   " Hush,
Speak not," said Dora, " now be wise ;
   Lie down, nor into danger rush."

" Let one advance," a harsh voice cried,
   Come doubly quick or I will fire."
" I come ! " a gentle voice replied,
   " Upon a woman wreak your ire ;
From brave men, helpless women fear
   No harm—I trust there's none in you."
" Strange, strange, indeed, the voice I hear,"
   His soft reply—" most strange, but true."

" I know those voices," quoth Leflore,
   " But do not understand."   " Nor I,"
Quoth Dora.   " Hush ! pull, pull ashore !
   There seem to be two parties nigh.

It must be so—the ferry this—
  Yours to the left—mine to the right—
And each in sore confusion is :
  Perchance we yet may make our flight."

"Nay, nay!" again the harsh voice cries :
  "Come in, I tell you, or I'll fire."
The soldier stood before their eyes,
  It was too late now to retire.
"We have surrendered," quoth Leflore,
  "Put down your gun—you dare not shoot."
"I'll be the first to step ashore."
  Quoth Dora, "and defy the brute."

'Twas marvelous strange—most pleasing so—
  Leflore was captured by his own.
A yell of joy went up—but, lo!
  Another yell of fiercer tone ;
Down came the fiercer boys in gray,
  Up went the sturdy boys in blue :
Tho' few the foes—most fierce the fray,
  The former, overpowered, withdrew.

Back to the mountains fled the gray ;
  Three of their bravest leaving there—
Two dead and one sore wounded lay,
  His sword still flashing in the air.

And wild with anguish Dora knew
  Her jealous lover, Ap Dahlgreen ;
At her in scorn his sword he threw,
  And bowed his face upon the green.

*   *   *   *   *   *   *   *

The scene is changed.   'Tis midnight hour,
And in a deep secluded bower,
Leflore and Ap Dahlgreen are met—
The former in his saddle set,
In all a gallant soldier's pride,
The latter standing at his side,
Emaciate, feeble, yet as proud,
His eye as fierce, his head unbowed.
" I come to take you to your own
Before your coming forth is known ;
'Tis whispered in our camp today,
Soon as you move to get away,
That open is the dungeon door
To close upon you," quoth Leflore.
Thus said, he leaped upon the green
And gave the reins to Ap Dahlgreen.
" Why should I fly ? What should I fear ?"
Quoth Ap Dahlgreen with angry tone,
" As long as I be peaceful here,
Will not brave men leave me alone ?
——4

Would not my flight suspicion wake
In those who trust me for your sake,
And turn their vengeance on my men?
Now guarded in your prison pen,
And held like brutes and felons there;
Forced oft your vile insults to bear
To gratify some coward's grudge;
Threatened with hanging if they budge
You captured them in open fight,
And each demand a soldier's right.
And does he get it?—tell me, pray—
See how they sicken day by day;
Those white-haired fathers, patriot's true,
Who to their shrines and fires renew
Their vows more fervently the more
You bathe them with their children's gore;
The firmer are their heart's alarms
The more they hear your clanking arms,
The more you taunt them, when you list,
The more with hatred they resist.
You fought from bushes—so did they.
You chose the method of affray.
You threw the gauntlet down, and now
A fair exchange will not allow.
My people driven to despair
Will not, cannot, must not forbear;

That thing called fear they dare not show,
The consequence none could forego—
They have been masters from their birth—
Their coming in and going forth
Has been in freédom and in pride,
And none but yours have such denied.
Now see them yonder in your power
Defamed—maltreated—hour by hour,
Yet none—not one—your pardon prays,
You cannot teach them abject ways.
They cannot bow the head or knee,
Not even though it set them free.
They'd rather perish than be mean,
Our men are men," quoth Ap Dahlgreen.

"It was my bullet, brought you low,
And on me with reacting blow
The missive struck. You know not why
I've heard your moans with pitying sigh,
I've borne your scorn without annoy,
Your convalescence hailed with joy ;
I've tried to soothe my captive's thrall,
And kept you from the prison wall.
So here again with you I plead ;
Come, ask not why, but take my steed ;
Unquestioning go forth tonight,

And wait not for the morning's light;
For then a guard will hold your door—
Now heed my warning," quoth Leflore.

" And so you counsel me to break
My true parole for safety sake.
You surely seeing me so rough
And simple, do not know the stuff
I'm made of—honor is to me
Priceless; what care I to be free
Without it.   Death, when it is gone,
I pray some power to hasten on.
I ask again what should I fear;
What charges dark 'gainst me appear?"

" Ab, there are whispers in the air,
And some are ready to declare
You massacred, one April morn,
Five men of ours, all travel worn,
Their armor cast aside for rest.
The act, they say, you have confessed,
But be this true or not, the blame
Lies at your door and flouts your claim
To mercy at our hands—so fly
And stay not, charges to deny;
Through me you hold your freedom—go!"

"My honor you cannot bestow,
When I have given it to you ;
You've been a friend, indeed, 'tis true ;
But my parole you did not grant.
With lifted eye, as is my wont,
I gave this to your armies—nay,
I've pledged my honor—here I'll stay.
Not only in the sight of men
I've pledged me o'er and o'er again,
But in the sight of God, and now
Can I unpunished break that vow,
And thus dishonor all my race?
Bring shame upon my father's face ?
I fear not charges vile—their power
Can never make me guiltless cower :
Compared with that large pledge of mine,
Made as it were at heaven's shrine.
Your force is but a gossamer,
My vow a cable chain as 'twere.
Others might do as you request
When sorely tempted, fiercely pressed,
Forget their honor for the while,
And thus preserve a carcass vile.
I will not—nay, I will not budge
Beyond my bounds—heaven be my judge."

"Discretion is the better part
Of valor—this we know ' by heart.'
Expediency, when passions rage,
Is best betimes, till they assuage.
Men oft do things they would not do,
And carry thus a purpose through ;
Forsake their rectitude awhile,
Some evil 'gainst themselves to foil.
But by remorse both dark and keen,
Are forced to wash their scutcheon clean,
And forced to keep it so—such men
Ne'er do those evil deeds again.
You seem presumptuous unto me ;
Why should you purer, better be,
Than these your fellows ?   Not one whit;
You're but a braver hypocrite."

" You waste your breath and argument,
Till winning conscience's assent,
    I will not copy after men
        Nor yield me to their beck and nod ;
    Save that behind them, there and then,
        I think I see the will of God.
  Our captains, when the kettle beats,
        Command, ' Fall in,' and we obey ;
    That order comes from sovereign seats

And not from them, poor things of clay.
That banner which I bear to death
  Is but a rag whose threads I spun,
My only courage, being faith,
  I cry therein, ' Thy will be done.'
Yon judge upon the bench is but
  A worm like me, and yesterday
He played with me about the hut,
  And went with me, perchance, astray.
But now he holds a sovereign seat,
  He holds a place of awful trust ;
He sits him at the Master's feet,
  Which give a glory to his dust.
He has the Master's Book in hand :
  I call him sire, he calls me son,
And I rise up at his command,
  And through him say, ' God's will be done.'
What makes me doff my hat to him—
  What makes me heed his frown and nod ?
As angry, why is he so grim ?
  He sits a servant there of God.
  I fawn not as a menial vile,
Nor from his frown as mortal run,
  But back of him I see a smile,
And feel I'm blest when that is won.
So when I see the law, I try

For peace and honor's sake, to find
Heartfelt obedience, and to tie
　My faith to it with steadfast mind.
'Tis not the letter of the law,
　Which I by schemes may break or shun :
The spirit of it gives me awe,
　That spirit cries, 'God's will be done.'"

" Once more I answer, Ap Dahlgreen,
I scorn your sermon and your spleen ;
What, if my men be wrought upon,
And fasten on you as the one,
Who, like a coward, vilely shot
Our general, lying on his cot ;
Begging for mercy ?　Now, I swear,
For your destruction they prepare ;
Since foes you have, and tales they tell,
Which mark you scarcely worthy hell.
Mark well my words, then, Ap Dahlgreen,
And take them just for what they mean :
Tomorrow, if they find you here,
　A dungeon's cell—a felon's fate—
Awaits you ; for upon my ear
　Still strikes their curse—their hiss of hate.
But if you still unaltered prove,
And misinterpret deeds of love,

And quite forget the risk I take
In breaking picket for your sake :
If still my warning true you scorn—
Hush ! hush ! that is the gathering horn ;
One hour from this will be too late—
Begone !   Nay, nay ! still obdurate ?
Then hear me and believe me, too,
Our lady has no love for you."
" It is a lie ; a foul, vile lie,"
Was Ap Dahlgreen's unkind reply.
" Draw not your pistol or your sword,
They could not kill me like your word.
You have strange graces ; I have none ;
A magnet has your voice's tone,
And I believe your courage true,
And think you patriotic, too ;
But you are not a friend of mine,
While in her eyes you try to shine,
And you that coat must cast aside
Ere she or I in you confide ;
No matter what your charms may be,
You are a traitor still to me.
And as a myrmidon of hate
And robbery, we'll ne'er abate
Our just antipathy for you,
And vainly at her shrine you'll woo.

Your smiles are insults, and your prayers
Are worthy only scornful stares ;
I'll give you access to her shrine,
With all your glory let you shine ;
I fear you not—nor feel alarm —
About your strange magnetic charm."

" I have been patient, still am so,
And have not triumphed as your foe ;
I've tempted you—you heard me not,
I've saved you from the captive's lot.
You've paid me up with insult—now,
Because she begs it, I allow
By army orders, you to go
In just exchange for me, and so
I give you till the sun is up
To get across yon mountain's top ;
And for your passport to your own,
This paper may be freely shown.
My outposts know the writing, and
Will give you safety through the land
As far as they may dare. I feel
That you will never break the seal,
But take it to the lady fair,
Whom you unasked my foe declare.
Then, fare you well, my friend—my foe—

Heaven keep you where you stay or go."
Like wild Comanche up he sprung
Himself, into his saddle flung,
And toward the mountain spurred his steed
With something of a Tartar's speed.
But Ap Dahlgreen stood half amazed,
And half in doubt and wholly dazed.
" Now for the mountain top," he cried,
" And first of all to Dora's side;
And then in time if Heaven be pleased
John Dacre, too, shall be released."

LEFLORE TO DORA.

What do I hear of thee,
   Ah, loveliest and most loved, so sad and low
And agonized in part by me,
   My sympathy is woe;
      And from the caverns of my breast,
      Its waters, like the ocean's yeast,
      Are lifted by a storm of sighs,
      And tears resistless flood mine eyes.

Ah, could I now be there,
   I weep because I cannot, and I fain
Would tell some sweet bird of the air
   My unremitting pain;

And bid it listen to my sighs,
And mark the hot tears of mine eyes,
And these for love and pity's sake,
Straight to thy spirit, sweet, to take.

What, though an exile from
Thy door, and may be only in thy scorn
I claim a place—most cruel doom,
In silence to be borne.
Yet let me say I would be blest,
Could I but send into thy breast
One joy, and doing thy command
Could I but daily touch thy hand.

I'd be so gay and bright,
  'Twould chase, methinks, thy pain and gloom away,
And leave thy heart lapp'd in the light
  Of cheer's benignant ray.
    As are the grasses lapped, when spring
    Soft folds the land beneath her wing,
    Which gleams so warm as 'twere at noon,
    From the golden bath tub of the sun.

Thy heart, it may be, shut
  Against my love so coldly as thy door
Is 'gainst my foot's instrusion, but
  Love leaps all barriers o'er ;

Its will and wings are strong and free,
And hasten o'er the stormiest sea,
Swift as the swiftest meteor
And weary not of journeying far.

Cheer up and give us joy ;
  Methinks the stars are brighter when they look
Upon thy face, in whose clear eye,
    As clear as clearest brook,
      The fiery thought unsullied gleams,
      The love-light plays like fairy dreams,
      The pure emotion, radiant swells,
      And truth's own fountain upward wells.

Cheer up, the flowers bloom
  The brighter for the smiles which thou hast given,
And send their kisses of perfume,
    Whose sweets they stole from heaven ;
      In answer to those sweetest eyes,
      Whose angels come from Paradise ;
      At these fair portals of the shrine
      Of thy fair soul, to sit and shine.

An altar there to claim—
  And why not ? For within my love-witched eyes
Methinks thine image's sweet flame,
    Sunlike doth set and rise.

Then why should not the perfect flowers,
Which are the soul eyes of the bowers,
Thus send their incense up to thee
And bathe thee in perfumery ?

What though all joyous things—
  All things of beauty, glory or delight,
As we must learn—be born with wings,
  Which prophesies their flight.
    Such as the radiance of the child,
    The spells of bliss—the raptures wild,
    The hues of buds—the charms of song—
    Which be too sweet to linger long.

Yet granting this ; for thee
  Fast as one joy forsakes, should come another,
And like a jeweled rosary
  Be knitted to each other ;
    Each in its turn to have its spell
    And fascination, to compel
    Gloom's ev'ry evil ling'ring sprite,
    From thy pure heart to take its flight.

Cheer up ! I pine for thee ;
  My heart for thee as often wildly thrills,
As shine the stars upon the sea,
  Or dance upon the rills.

With sighs my waking thoughts begin,
And oh, these thoughts of thee are sin,
Because of their idolatry ;
But, sweet, they're full of prayer for thee.

Must all my prayers be vain—
Vain as the last sweet notes that one awakes
Of some inexplicably witching strain
Before the good shell breaks.
Love's is that strain, so rich and rare,
Which must itself in part declare
By leaping from my heart—the lute—
Ere breaking quite and waxing mute.

When once it breaks, its chords
May ne'er be tuned to any song again ;
Henceforth they'll echo but such words
As breathe of woe and pain.
Yet may this song—this tristful rhyme,
When vanished has thy summer prime,
In the winter of grief's years,
Awaken yet some mem'ry's tears.

Then, not in vain shall be
These echoes of love's waters running o'er—
Pride's barriers—sighing after thee,
Their ocean evermore.

And still, I hope, that not all vain
Shall prove the mournings of this strain,
For love as yet ne'er breathed a word
Which was not of some fond heart heard.

“ Your sarvant, sir,” said she, approaching
  The guard at the dark prison door.
“ I hopes dat I is not encroachin’,
  For I means you no harm, to be shure.

“ You see, ef dis place is de prison
  For de rebels, my massa is here,
And dese clothes in dis basket is his’n,
  And I thought ef de cap’n don’t keer,

“ I’ll fotch ’em to him—dat’s to massa—
  And ’low him to change—don’t you see ?
And I says, ef de cap’n jest says so,
  His sarvant I’m sartain to be.”

“ No, madam, the dirty old rebel
  May keep on his lousy old clothes ;
He’s so anxious to get into trouble
  He’ll get but his dues, I suppose.”

——5

“ But, sir, spite of dat, if you know him,
　　He’s praying for peace all de day,
And hit looks like de angels came to him,
　　And fetch what he wants when he pray.

“ As for bein’ a rebel, I ’scuse him—
　　A good man will stand by his kin ;
As for lice, sir, dey wouldn’t amuse him,
　　No filth ken dey find on his skin.

“ Shucks man, all de quality show him,
　　Like us niggers, dere bounden respects ;
Bress your soul, hits a fact, you don’t know him—
　　He’s clean as de Bible directs.

“ You’uns got it all wrong when you doubt him,
　　Ole massa is white to de core,
And you need’n’ say nuffin about him,
　　You’uns never have seed him afore.

“ His darkies, you ax ’em, dey love him,
　　A rebel, indeed ! what of dat ?
He’s good, but you nebber must shove him —
　　He’ll fight at de drop of a hat.

“ La, man, lemme go wid de basket,
　　Lemme take up ole massa de clothes,

In de name of young missus I ask it ;
　　You'uns know she's a lady, I 'spose."

" He isn't your master—no matter
　　How good the old rebel may be ;
To you and your folks we are better,
　　We've come here to set you all free.

" He isn't your master, and never
　　Shall call you his slave anymore ;
Your fetters are broken forever,
　　The days of your bondage are o'er.

" Lor' bress you, on which er percasion
　　Dis matter I can't argify,
When we takes in de whole situation
　　We sees wid a different eye.

" I knows when I talks to my betters,
　　In dis, sir, de nigger's no fool ;
You'uns talk now of mighty big matters
　　To one what hain't been to no skule.

" But I picks up a heap round de table,
　　I learns wid my eyes and my ears,
My quality folks nebber gabble,
　　Hits wisdom dey talks and I hears.

"De white man am master, de nigger
   Is servant by habit and force,
When de white man gits bigger and bigger
   De nigger fares better, encourse.

" Nigger works for de feller what feeds him,
   You does jest the same, sir, I s'pose.
Nigger follows de feller what leads him,
   Jes so, sir, wid you'uns, I knows.

" One man he is born to be master,
   'Tother man he is born 'tother way,
And togedder dey sticks like a plaster,
   No matter what you'uns may say.

" I sticks to de people what knows me,
   Dere home is my home, don't you see;
My labor and duty dey shows me,
   I does it, and den I am free.

" My missus she pet me and praise me—
   House-keeping turns ober to me,
From de field to de parlor she raise me,
   And gib me de lock and de key.

" De keys to de cubbard, does missus,
   De keys to de smoke-house likewise,

And she hand me de keys to de presses,
    What seeing would 'stonish you' eyes.

Shucks ! I knows whar I is—how I got dar—
    And knows when you gimme de bread,
Which side has been kivvered wid butter,
    Shoo, man, does you hear what I said ?"

" Young missus ! ole massa ! all devils !
    Get on with your basket—get on,
They beat you with broom sticks and shovels,
    Then, cur-like, upon them you fawn."

" Well, master or not—makes no matter,
    Lemme take him dese clothes—for you see
Dat's de onliest thing I is atter,
    You mustn't keep talking to me."

" All right, then—remember, I am ready
    To lead you from bondage away.
After while we can make you a lady,
    No master to fear or obey.

" After while you can ride in a carriage,
    And travel in freedom and ease,
Some white man may take you in marriage,
    And then you can do as you please.

" You'll sit in your parlor at leisure,
   And order your servants around,
And white girls may find it a pleasure
   To sit at your feet on the ground."

" Hush man ! don't you see I'se a nigger?
   And nebber expec's, in my day,
To cut in dis worl' sich a figger—
   I calls dat a-going astray.

" 'Sides dis you mout git into worry,
   And sometime be needing a friend,
And den you'd be terrible sorry,
   Your kindness you didn't extend.

" Dem mountains is chuckful of rebels,
   And what ef dey catch you some day,
And young missus should hear of your troubles,
   Her kindness I knows you would pray.

" Hits gospel I talks, and my 'suasion,
   Hits good for de soul as a smile,
If you help me on which erpercashion,
   I may help you a bit atterwhile."

" Your head, as the boys say, is level;
   I'll grant what you ask—but you see

It's done for your sake—that old devil
  Can't get any favors from me."

Up, up to the cell, where the master
  Stood listening to all that was said,
Went this woman whom social disaster
  The slave of another had made.

And casting her bundle before him,
  And shaking him glad by the hand,
Respectful she stood to assure him,
  Her service was at his command.

Piece by piece from the basket, the linen
  Was spread on the bench at the door,
With chatting, and chuckling, and grinning,
  And calling their names, o'er and o'er.

" Dey are talking down yonder of rebels,
  Of killing some people, I knows,—
Of shooting and hanging de debbels,
  You know who dey talk of, I 'spose.

" A horse by de spring in de bushes
  Am waiting—you git him and ride—
And a ' dug out ' am hid in de rushes
  Where de ribber is rocky and wide.

“ Dat window’s right high ’bove de water,
    But high is de tree by de wall ;
And a brave man can jump, and he orter
    If he knows what I knows—dat is all.

“ Dis ball is right rough, but no matter
    Hits use atter while you can larn,
Young missus she sont you a letter
    I kivers hit over wid yarn.

“ Well, bress you, good-bye ; I must hurry
    Old miss mout be waiting for me ;
’Bout hanging and shooting, don’t worry,
    By morning I specs you’ll be free.”

        *   *   *   *   *   *   *   *

She went as she came, and the shadows
    Came down as she passed from the doors,
But the light seemed to shine on the meadows
    Much longer than ever before.

To the old man much longer than ever
    The twilight remained ; and the night,
And the darkness of darkness, seemed never
    A going to shut out the light.

Impatient he nervously listens,
    While gazing far out on the vale,
Where the waterfall gushes and glistens
    And the whip-poor-will chirrups her tale.

He listens for footfalls and voices
    Of guards as they march to their post :—
In vain, and his spirit rejoices
    That a mist fills the vale like a ghost.

The ash tree, it touches his window,
    His fellows lie sleeping around
And none are to question or hinder—
    'Tis forty feet down the ground.

The twine, it is doubled—thrice twisted—
    And tied to the bolt of the door :
Then by guards he would not be molested
    While he swung from his cell, if no more.

"If it snap, it is then even better,"
    Quoth he, "than to die here in chains,
Or released for a while from the fetters
    To know that the halter remains.

" And the halter, oh, horrors ! poor Dora,
    Bereft and heart-broken must be ;

May the angels of mercy watch o'er her
    And keep her. Poor Dora! Poor me!"

He swings at the end of his tether,
    A stout branch he seizes—it bends,
But a stouter is caught—then another.
    So safe to the trunk he descends.

But a moment he listening pauses,
    The waterfall only is heard :—
A figure the bridge noiseless crosses
    And startles the night plaining bird.

"No harm there," quoth he, quick descending :
    'Tis Fanny's, the figure he sees ;
She speechless before him is bending
    And clasping in rapture his knees.

"Now fly, Massa, fly ; in de alley
    Ole Barny he's hitched : must make haste,
Jest follow de mist of de valley,
    No time now 'fore morning to waste."

"Good-bye"—"bye you bye"—thus they parted ;
    And a mocking bird chirped in the spray :
"Good omen," quoth he, as he darted
Thro' the mist down the streamlet away.

The scene is changed.   By Fennell's fount
At noon there is a hurried mount
Of six guerillas ; at the call
Ot one just 'scaped from prison wall.
" A score of men are after me
But tow'rds the lower Tennessee
Their horses heads are turned," said he.
" And I'm persuaded, too, that spies
Are here and there in nice disguise,
Both white and black, who know me well,
Too glad my hiding place to tell ;
And even now a troop, I learn,
Awaits the old man's slow return.
Now, let me tell you ere you go,
That is a gallant, fighting foe ;
Their prowess 'tis not well to scorn,
And you may learn this ere the morn."
" All right," one burly youngster says,
" You seek the shortest route to ' Fez,'
I went there once upon a time
With Ap Dahlgreen—we had to climb
The mountains to avoid the Yanks,
Who played just then most vengeful pranks,
On everything that wore the gray,
In each imaginable way.
Because they'd given too big a dare

To some of ours who wouldn't scare
At everything that made a noise,
And just about a dozen boys,
Their bravest ones, of course—alas!
Got butchered in a mountain pass."
" Alas! you say ' alas !' Why, boy ?"
Says old John Dacre, with annoy ;
" I wish their army had been there,
Their fate and worse than it to share.
But what you say is very true,
The devil's got into the Blue.
I know, if anybody knows,
To what extent his vengeance goes.
Who'll guide me down the Hurricane,
Avoiding every field and lane,
Across the bottom to the grot
Where Johnson made that noble shot,
Which set so many horses free
And, by the way, gave two to me ?"—
" And to your servant this good gray."
Another said, " I know the way."
" Who knows the pathway, rude and rough,
That leads up tow'rds the topmost bluff ?"
John Dacre asks : " When there I come
I'm, as the saying goes, at home.
I wish to chat with Farley there.

Farley's a hermit in his lair,
A very curious man and wise,
That shuts his mouth and opes his eyes;
From him we'll get our bearings true,
And learn exactly what to do."
A cavalier, with eye so keen,
Who had been silent hitherto,
Here answers: " 'Twas with Ap Dahlgreen
I climbed the mountain by the moon—
Ride not to be forgotten soon—
And in that ride we chanced to stop
With Farley of the mountain top."
" Move forward then, my gallants ! move !
Your gallantry this night approve."
" I'll lead you," quoth John Dacre, " where
Horses and saddles are to spare."
Not long their ride from Fennell's fount
Across the bottoms to the mount,
Tho' twilight caught them at the foot,
Each pressing on a foaming brute.
" Dismount and lead," 'twas said—'twas done,
The climbing slope on slope begun,
When a murmur on the night air swells
Of horsemen on the highway tells.
" 'Twas this I feared," John Dacre said ;
" Yet see that little light ahead

From Farley's door; it gleams afar
Across the shadows like a star.
" Ah, now," cried he, with eye so keen,
" For forty men and Ap Dahlgreen
I'd learn those riders' mission here,
And teach them night time raids to fear."
The sounds died out, and up and on
With weary limbs, but nerve and brawn,
Both man and horse ascend at last;
" Thank heaven !" John Dacre sighs, " 'tis past.
The night has only just begun,
We'll reach my home with easy run;
But Farley hail," 'twas said—'twas done.
He stands the weary squad before :
" How is it, friend," the greeting o'er—
" How is it with you here tonight ?
Your candle, with its star-like light,
Has been to us a glorious guide,
And more, a thing of cheer beside."
Quoth Farley, " Only yesterday
A force of blue coats came this way,
But came not to my solitude,
'Tis said a rebel they pursued.
They pass this summit cot of mine,
And give no courtesy to its shrine.
Perchance—what else I cannot guess—

It stands so white and neighborless.
As 'twere a ghost they let it pass :
But what is this you do ? " " Alas !
The fates are rather rough on me—
I am the rebel they pursue
For doing what all men should do—
Defending home and self. Last spring
I gave them buckshot on the wing,
And one of theirs was left with me—
A braver man you never see—
I shot him—cured him "—" Yes, I know,"
Quoth Farley, " yes, he told me so."
" He told you ?" queried Dacre, " what ?
And who was he that told you that ?"
" Leflore, of course," quoth Farley ; " see,
Here is a note he left with me
Some weeks ago. I thought it then,
A trick to get me in his den,
And fancied in each line a snare.
Why should he have so nice a care
For one who shot him, as he said,
From ambush, when his henchmen fled.
At any rate, I kept the note,
Thinking I'd have it yet to quote
Against him, should he pounce on me
And take me in captivity,

For giving aid and comfort here
To you and yours. But take the queer
And unique warning that he sent,
And read it to your heart's content."

THE LETTER.

John Dacre, you have deadly foes ;
For 'round your very home are those
Who, in your torment, take delight,
And now would sell your head for spite,
You are a traitor, in a sense,
And in the changes of events,
Some sad mishap may so befall,
As yet to fill your cup with gall.
Now, if this ended in yourself,
Made silent by a little pelf,
It would not matter much—but so
It would not happen--for the blow
That strikes you down, beyond you flies
And brings another heart to sighs—
Another heart so pure, so true,
So brave, so kind—with sins so few,
Methinks 'twould anger earth and heaven
If wounds to such a heart were given.
And while I have an arm, I'll fight
In her behalf, or wrong or right,

With ready, sweet, good will ; for, sir,
I know I'd give my life for her,
For there's in me beyond—above—
My patriotism another love ;
And 'tis, as I to you confess,
Love for a perfect loveliness,
Such as I have not found elsewhere
Save in your daughter, and I dare
Remind you, that I never drew
This holy sentiment from you,
Or at your instigation, sir ;
I got tuition but from her —
Hers is the magic-like divine
Which has transformed this life of mine.
Your opposition I deplore,
Because I know it hurts her sore,
And adds new madness to a strife
Now with unnatural hate too rife.
And know you—if you know it not—
Albeit I have cast my lot
With those who fight for Union and
The integrity of all the land,
I am a Southron, and I fight
Secession with a mad delight.
But be this as it may be, we
On theories cannot agree.
——6

I own my obligations now
To you and yours, but still allow
One who can ne'er your acts forget,
To be a greater debtor yet,
And this enclosure take to her
As a poor heart's remembrancer.

LINES TO DORA.

If I should scrawl a simple verse,
Your faults or praises to rehearse,
And neither be verbose or terse,
          Nor yet sing song,
Simply for better or for worse,
          Would it be wrong?

All correspondence you forbid,
Your thought and feeling you'd keep hid,
And thus your haughty mem'ry rid
          Of dreams of passion.
What harm for me to lift the lid
          In tuneful fashion?

What harm if I should break the spell
Of reticence you've spun so well,
In which your sweet self seems to dwell
          A cloistered nun ?

What harm to peep into your cell
    In very fun ?

Methinks 'twould be a pleasing art
To touch with humor's harmless dart,
The tearful darkness of your heart,
    And for awhile
Mirth's witching glory to impart,
    And make it smile.

Methinks I'd be a friend, indeed,
Come in the very nick of need
If, when the thoughts and feelings bleed
    In sad neglect,
A balm, with this my tuneful reed,
    I could inject.

Perchance 'twould be a mercy shown,
To make you feel the less alone,
And by some touch—some look—some tone—
    To startle you ;
In Spring-time thus the bud is blown
    By sun and dew.

To be remembered is so sweet ;
It has the joy of angels' feet,
Of music from a dismal street,

Of childhood's mirth,
Of glances soft when lover's meet,
          And of spring-kiss'd earth.

To be remembered when forlorn
We silent weep and silent mourn,
It comes grief's Baal to overturn,
          And by fact to prove
That there's a balm from Gilead borne,
          And that God is love.

So my heart's love remembers you,
It scatters sorrow's precincts through
As charity's sweet sisters do;
          Not what it wants,
But what it needs, like sun and dew
          To tristful haunts.

Yes, my poor heart forgets you not,
But keeps your image unforgot,
And begs no sweeter, happier lot
          Than at your side,
Whether in palace or in cot
          To beat and bide.

There like puissant cavaliers
I'd scorn alike man's praise and jeers,

And from the mystery of the years—
    To pledges true—
Would weave a madrigal of tears
    Or smiles for you.

Now, whether from my heart to yours
Love makes his hourly, daily tours,
To pay to you his fond devoirs,
    It matters not;
Content he'll hang about your doors
    And bear his lot.

But I forget me somewhat, when
I took in hand my rhyming pen
I did not think I'd talk again
    So solemnly,
Only to make you, now and then,
    Remember me.

I thought I'd write of pleasant things,
And show my fancy's rollickings,
As flying on her swift, bright wings,
    Now here, now there,
She plays upon life's treble strings
    A merry air.

As 'tis—and as it is, 'tis best—
I fling these fancies at you, lest
You chance to think that with the rest
      I you forget;
Nay—you've the night key of my breast
      And room here yet.

   *   *   *   *   *   *   *   *

But, ere I close, in chief I write
To bid you be on guard at night,
And not for one night only, but
For weeks one eye you must not shut;
For some there be who hate you sore—
Who get admission to your door.
Now Ap Dahlgreen no longer roams,
No longer keeps them in their homes,
They rob and plunder us and you:
Now they are gray—now they are blue—
The thief, in times like these, you see,
Makes good his opportunity.
Peace dulls the assassin's deadly knife,
But it is sharpened well by strife.
I'd rather have you there, and know
You kept these scoundrels hiding low,
Than have you bound in chains, while they
Unchecked make all of us a prey.

Further than this I cannot say.
Verbum sap sat : the maxim goes,
And though we still are civic foes,
And deal all honorable blows
Each to the other—'tis but fair
That arms like gentlemen we bear,
Nor strike in ambush, and not smite
A man when flat down in the fight.

Thus ran his letter : "Had I thought,"
Quoth Farley, "that the fellow sought
To shield you"—"Never mind, my friend,"
John Dacre added, "for the end
Had been the same, for I, like you,
Would ne'er have deemed his purpose true.
Mine is a long, long tale of woe.
I need not tell—you need not know :
Sufficient when they came again
I lay a-fevered, racked with pain.
This mattered not to them nor me ;
I scorned their pity—scorned to see
Their gentle graces to my child,
Whom they left desolate in the wild ;
For her alone I would have prayed,
The poor, benighted, love lorn maid,
That I with her and she with me

Might share the same captivity,
That she might learn thereby some hate,
Her strange love to obliterate,
That bound in filthy prison pen
Hearing the curses of their men,
This as a poison slow but sure,
That other poison—death—might cure.
I felt like praying this—but no,
I could not give my child a blow;
Cheerful the steed they brought I strode,
And mutely to my prison rode.
You see me here—you see these men—
You see before us in yon glen
A daring outpost—they are bold—
Leflore commands it, I am told.
He roams in gay impunity
Since Ap Dahlgreen's no longer free,
And him with tortured mind and soul
Binds with the cobweb of parole.
Tonight without or fraud or ruse,
We aim to let his prisoner loose,
If fighting fierce and riding hard
Can bring this captive his reward.

The scene is changed.   From day to day,
In listless stupor, Dora lay ;
And night by night, for two dark weeks,
Her fancy played the wildest freaks,
And images of grief and pain
Seemed ever flitting through her brain.
By day her thoughts she could not wean
From Ap Dahlgreen, good Ap Dahlgreen ;
As twilight came, with mutterings lower,
And weird, soft, 'twas "my Leflore "—
And ever and anon by night,
With look of pleading and affright
'Twas, "oh, my father, hear! I pray,"
Until the fever passed away.
The last was chained in felon's cell,
The first lay bleeding where he fell,
Till cared for by a gen'rous foe
With all the kindness friends bestow,
Go forth unfettered on parole,
And, to the promptings of his soul,
Obedient seeks his lady's bower
In time to foil the fever's power.
And, though himself but half alive,
Is strong to watch and wait and strive
With evils worse than his or hers ;

For Love a giant's will confers ;
So many a day and many a night,
With all the softness of a sprite,
He keeps his sentry at her side—
(Her black nurse eyeing him with pride,
Or silent weeping in despair,
Or venting song-like, dirge-like prayer)—
He keeps his sentry patient, true,
While Dora scarce his presence knew.
The fever passes.   Reason's light
Comes like the fair dawn after night,
Its glory now begins to shine
Brighter than overbrimming wine,
In each rich lineament of her face;
And soon he fancies he can trace
A timid awkwardness each day,
A constant effort to be gay,
Albeit the soft sighs of her breast
Declare her spirit ill at rest
While he sits by her.   In his heart
Pride half rebels and says, " Depart."
For he has learned—'twas hard to learn
While yet his suit she could not spurn,
His pleadings but increased her care—
Alas ! he was not welcome there,
His love's wild dream must prove all vain,

His hope must end in madding pain.
As he took counsel with despair,
Her presence he could scarcely bear,
His manliness in compass rose,
His heart with other fervor glows.

* * * * * * * *

A budget from his breast he drew.
To honor's tryst he had been true,
And ne'er had broke the seal; yet sore
The trial—'twas from her Leflore.
Nor did he break the seal—yet felt
The thrusts each hidden utt'rance dealt:
His spirit's eyes could almost read
The words which made his spirit bleed.
But with this in his hand he bore
The trust and passport of Leflore.
But stronger claim than this, forsooth,
He was a man, and one of truth.
He hides it in his breast again,
Where 'gainst it beats his heart with pain.

* * * * * * * *

The midnight stars above her meet,
And soft she lies in slumber sweet,
And full orbed through her lattice glows

The moon, to mellow her repose;
And o'er her radiant face the light
Of sweet dreams come and take their flight;
Yet long enough even there remain
To brush away each hint of pain.
Her soft guitar he wakes, and flings
His soul into the song he sings :

DREAM ON, FAIR GIRL.

Dream on, fair girl, through all this night,
　　And for this while forget
To weep and sigh : the stars so bright
　　To smile on thee are met.
Let friendship's garlands from thy shrine,
　　Love's homage be withdrawn,
Those faithful stars for thee will shine : —
　　Dream on, fair girl, dream on.

Dream on, fair girl, could stars declare
　　My burning thoughts to thee,
Or whisper to thy soul my prayer,
　　Most blest thy dreams would be.
As Eve's of heaven were, when first
　　She breathed, she saw the dawn,
But thou'dst not know like her the worst,
　　But sinless, pure, dream on.

Dream on, fair girl, thy blessed lips,
  On which I fancy lies
The tints, which Flora, in her trips
  Between the earth and skies,
Spilt affluent on thy faultless mouth,
  And with the dews of dawn,
Warmed by the kisses of the South,
  Diluted them.   Dream on.

Dream on, fair girl, and smile the same :
  I know some angel's kiss
Is kindling in thy heart a flame
  Unknown to wakefulness.
Even from thy lashes comes its flash,
  As from darkness comes the dawn,
In golden raiment sweet and fresh
  From chambers warm ; dream on.

Dream on, fair girl, and from the moon,
  Which through thy lattice plays,
May fortune catch some special boon
  With which to bless thy days ;
So that when night's sweet dreams prove vain,
  And their glories bright be gone,
Some heav'n-sent hope shall still remain—
  Dream on, sweet girl, dream on.

*   *   *   *   *   *   *   *

While yet his strains re-echo soft
Down river bank, up gorge aloft,
The tramp of iron hoofs is heard ;
The night hawk from his tree is stirred ;
The bark of cur—the deep-mouthed bay
Of hounds that watch the dark highway,
Startle the echoes far and near,
And thrill the spirit through the ear.
Instant one hand goes to his breast,
He draws a budget from his vest ;
The other to his pistol goes—
Ah, this a faithful friend he knows.
One horseman only comes—is near—
A thrill darts through him—'tis not fear.
He knows that horseman is Leflore,
Who needs must seek by night her door ;
He dares not venture here by day,
Too many foes beset the way :
And shall he fly—like dastard fly—
Or must the lone intruder die.
Ah, horrid thought—most torturing still—
A benefactor thus to kill ;
Yet is he not a deadly foe
To him and country—doubly so :

Foe to his poor heart's peace, and worse,
His people's unrelenting curse?
Yet horrid thought—'tis poltroon like.
And as assassins do, to strike
The bitterest enemy—foul deed
For which there was no potent need;
Yet, yet, he argues who would know
The hand that dealt the deadly blow?
Are not these paths each day beset
With ruthless riders, tireless yet?
Did not his troopers merciless
Right here their fancied wrongs redress,
And wreak uncivil vengeance here
On Dora and her sire—with sneer
And taunts insulting yesterday,
And captive take that sire away,
And drive her back, remorseless still?
What harm were there such foe to kill?
And who would blame him when 'twere known?
One brave invader was o'erthrown—
He were not to his country true.
And were he not a traitor, too,
To let one scourge—one tyrant pass—
When he could strike him down. Alas,
'Twould be assassination vile,
On which good angels could not smile,

And this would be upon his soul,
And all its memories control
And scorch it worse than fiery brand,
And blast its life forevermore.
'Twould stand a spectre in his door:
'Twould haunt his mem'ry like a cloud,
And all life long that life enshroud.
" My country's foe, " he cries, " and mine,
To others I this deed resign."

Nearer and nearer, slowly drew
The horseman to the gate; in yiew,
A hundred paces off, he reins
His weary, foaming steed—remains
Still-cautious in his saddle—eyes
The premises with care, and pries
Into a vacant cabin near;
And lists, perchance a step to hear—
And Ap Dahlgreen is watching, too.
Resolved to honor to be true,
He steals quick backward through the hall,
Though loud and clear seemed each footfall;
His nerves and muscles both had ears,
So keen and sharp became his fears :—
He leaps the barn yard fence—a cur
Snarls at him low, but does not stir.

He passes to the barn and—"bang"—
A gun shot on the night air rang.
There was a moment's silence—then
A horse goes flying up the glen.
Another and another shot,
A yell once heard, never forgot,
And then an old man's husky shout,
And "whiz" a bullet flies about
His ears, too fatal near—his steed
Is saddled, mounted, put to speed.
Alas, alas—too late, too late,
Some mounted pickets stood in wait;
These, thinking him the foe they sought,
Their guns upon him flying brought,
Six loud reports the silence break
And sixty shot his pathway rake.
The horse, receiving many a wound,
Reels, plunges headlong to the ground;
The rider stricken, too, is caught
Beneath the dead steed where he lies,
And there, to wild delirium brought
By loss of blood, in anguish dies.

*   *   *   *   *   *   *   *

——7

The scene is changed.   Again Leflore
Has fallen captive, wounded sore,
Again, a tender nursing knows,
Such as true chivalry bestows.
That manly and considerate care
John Dacre ever had to spare,
To all who at his mercy lay.
Again, and 'twas no evil day—
Sweet Dora like an angel smiled,
And half his agonies beguiled,
And half his ailments quite removed,
By kindness not to be reproved ;
For 'tis by doctoring the heart
We often cure the outer part.
And thus, while gloom upon him preyed,
A solace sweet her touch conveyed ;
Her coming was a ray of light,
Like that which cheers the dungeon's night.
The music of her voice's tone
Came to his heart like heaven's own.
'Twas common in those woeful days
The soldier sought the rude highways,
And came not back to make report
Of ventures wild or gallant sport.
Thus one by one, and two by two,

Went to return not, and none knew
Their bitter fate.   So cheap is life
When men accustomed grow to strife.
His men were gallant men and true,
As every fighting rebel knew ;
While for their country's cause they fought,
Not oftener than our men they sought,
Themselves from harm or death to shield,
Reckless they sought the battle field ;
Oft with chivalric nonchalance
Ventured into the darkest haunts.
They ceased to pillage when they knew
Their foes as patriots brave and true.
As times went by, each side began
To think the other one a man,
And scorned the braggart as a fool
Or blustering coward, as a rule.

*   *   *   *   *   *   *   *

But months roll on, and still Leflore
Can scarcely leave the cottage door.
His friends had vanished far away,
And here at length he needs must stay.
John Dacre put away his frown,
Upon him looked compassionate down,
And even begged of him a song

To cheer the winter nights so long.
Too glad was he - the captive—he,
The double captive, thus to see
The father's smile—too glad to hear
His words of sympathy and cheer;
'Twas inspiration to his heart,
And seemed new hope—life to impart.
So, gazing out upon the scene,
The new made mound of Ap Dahlgreen,
Before him in the moonlight lay.
His spectre round it seemed to stray,
And one sweet song that he had sung,
Which oft with jealous pangs had stung
His heart, and sunk into its core,
Now shook the mem'ry of Leflore.
The cause of jealous care removed,
His gen'rous soul the song approved;
So as a tribute to the foe,
Who always dealt an honest blow—
The martyr of a cruel war—
He seized my lady's sweet guitar,
And sang to her, his own heart's queen,
This sad song of dead Ap Dahlgreen.

AP DAHLGREEN'S SONG.

Yes, afterwhile—but only afterwhile—
  When I forget these cruel years,
Some Puck my poor heart may beguile,
  And seal its fount of tears,
      My sweet love.
From these wild dreams some nobler dreams create,
  And mem'ry's mastery overthrow,
And love rekindle—spite of fate—
  It may be so,
      My sweet love.

Yes, when I change—but only when I change—
  And know the mystery of these days,
And snatch from fancy's farthest range,
  The glory it displays,
      My sweet love.
Perchance with ease I'll bear my burden's weight,
  In heart and head I'll stronger grow ;
And learn love's sweetness—spite of fate—
  It may be so,
      My sweet love.

Yet well, full well I deem, that after years,
  My olden self to time will yield,

I'll know no more these bitter tears—
   These heart wounds will be healed,
               My sweet love.
Still shall remembrance lose her tablet then?
   May she a different record show?
Begin her doom's day book again?
   It may be so,
               My sweet love.

Then not in vain shall hope new colors spread,
   As ne'er were done by mortal art,
Nor shall she give us, begging bread,
   A stone unto the heart,
               My sweet love.
Old dreams and fancies may be used again,
   Their glory in a new dress show,
And love will rule a vesta, then,
   It may be so,
               My sweet love.

   *   *   *   *   *   *   *   *

   The sweet song ended, at his side
   Stands Dora, mute and mystified,
   And near her brave John Dacre stands,
   With pensive brow and folded hands.
   Leflore scarce saw them, but he felt

This song the father's heart must melt.
" Leflore, my boy," the old man said,
" Out yonder, 'neath the grass, lies dead
The noblest, bravest, gentlest youth,
That ever battled North or South.
He loved this child of mine, and I
Saw her repel him with a sigh ;
I blame her not.   'Tis heaven's decree,
And still an unsolved mystery,
The strange affinities of hearts.
Not all the deep and cunning arts
Of reason ever can detect,
Nor heart's dislikes, or likes direct.
Thus in all loving true, intense,
There is another unnamed sense,
Which is to Love, blind otherwise,
The keenest, most far-sighted eyes.
I go about the land to find
A hero pleasing to my mind ;
I do not search for him in vain,
He is a man of heart and brain ;
He is most beautiful in form,
And me his graceful motions charm,
I bring him to my daughter.   She
In him sees nothing that I see ;
His presence has no charm for her—

His arts cannot her spirits stir;
In him there's nothing to admire
And naught to kindle passion's fire,
Each tender, wooing word of his—
Each loving plea repulsive is
As turned her mother's eyes on me,
And I found favor in them—she
Has turned her charmed eyes on you :—
Wearing the color that you do
To me and her most hateful; but
To this her visual eyes seem shut.
Mine cannot be—but 'tis too late—
Too late and vain besides, 'gainst fate
To strive. Our gallant boys today
To all war's evils are the prey;
All but their deathless pluck is gone.
The world has left us all alone,
Not even pity sheds a tear
Above this fairest child that e'er
Was born in freedom's family.
The Southron's cause—the end I see.

*   *   *   *   *   *   *   *

Beside the darkly flowing wave
The stranger sees one lonely grave,
But in it slumber side by side

Three heroes once their country's pride.
Beneath one simple slab—whereon
Their names are cut, and when they died.
And o'er them is a myrtle crown,
Bestudded by three stars—that's all.
And often from the cottage hall,
Vine clad and beautiful and bright,
Two women come—one black, one white—
The former bowed with many years,
The latter bowed with many tears;
Come to the tomb, their Mecca shrine,
And there recall the days " Lang Syne."

IT WAS NOT ALL A DREAM.

Down where the Alabama flows,
Calm and deep as the pulse of those
Who see its fountain and its close,
  A mighty stream,
I lay me down to find repose—
  And I dreamed a dream.

'Twas in an April's sun I lay
To while my weariness away,
Waiting a steamboat from the bay;
  How could one dream
Of aught but glories on such a day,
  By such a stream?

The south winds bathed me with perfume,
And through the soft air's hazy gloom,
There stole a glow like a rose's bloom
  And kissed the trees,
And the earth in space seemed to rock and loom
  In radiant ease.

Yes, the earth, the sky, the air, the sea,
Seemed marvelous beautiful to me,
And splendor rode with minstrelsy,
    And peace with pride,
And chastity and chivalry
    Sat side by side.

And I saw upon a thousand plains,
Upon a thousand hills, white fanes,
And interspersed with waving grains
    Gold fruitage hung,
And up the byways and the lanes
    Came mirth and song.

And I heard afar the evening horn,
And from a thousand fields of corn,
And of bloomy cotton, soft was borne
    The minstrelsy
Of the negro riding tow'rds the barn,
    With weird glee.

Ah, the land of treasure knew no dearth ;
In pride and beauty, she went forth,
Like a maiden in her jewel'd girth,
    And crowned in flowers ;
Ah, this was the happiest land of earth,
    This land of ours.

And while I dreamed thus idlewise,
I saw a marvelous pageant rise—
A city's bases in the skies,
          Downward its towers,
But beautiful.as paradise,
          Reeling in flowers.

And wild, sweet song came from its streets,
And mirth like that when youth youth meets,
. And a rosy tide of odor sweets
          Came floating down,
And music charmed the dim retreats,
          Of that rare town.

There was neither mourn, nor wail, nor sigh,
Nor breath of storm, nor cloud in sky,
But the balmy peace of by and by,
          Its stars set forth,
To fill the world with glory—ay,
          To enchant the earth.

There was no shadow of despond,
Yet ever and anon beyond
The wondrous pageant, there waved a wand,
          That shook its base,
To which the welkin would respond
          With fiery face.

And farther still beyond, the hum
Of solemn sounds, the roll of drum,
The ring of steel, the howl of bomb,
  And into eclipse
The city's lights were thrown, and dumb
  Grew its joyous lips.

Strange mingling in one scene, the charms
Of peace-tide and the clank of arms,
The cheering horn and the alarms
  Of the trump and fife,—
The sweet mirth of the quiet farms,
  With the battle's strife.

For the rueful clank of arms I heard,
Which ev'ry pulse and vital stirred,
And horsemen hither, thither spurred,
  And footmen pale,
Quick or their loins their armor gird,
  And fill the vale.

I ask me what does this portend—
Subverted fabrics?　God forfend!
And can it prophesy an end
  Of glory's state?
Can't our Palladium strong withstand
  The assaults of hate?

While thus I wondered, full of awe,
Yet half enchanted at what I saw,
Without a rhyme or reason's law,
        A hand was seen,
Before my glaring eyes to draw
        A fiery screen.

And ever and anon there came
Portents of sorrow, grief and shame,
Shadows and types without a name,
        And mutterings low,
Of unseen storms, or of pent up flame,
        Like a volcano.

Then the pageant vanished, and the skies
Were full of moans, and clouds, and sighs,
And I saw an awful phantom rise—
        Awful and strong—
Yet in the lips, and brow, and eyes,
        There seemed no wrong.

In vain to close my eyes I tried—
To rise, to fly away and hide;
From such dread portents, 'twas denied.
        So, in despair,
To the bright phantom loud I cried:
        " In mercy, spare."

Then in a twinkling changed the scene,
And the tide of war rolled wild between
The epochs.   The fields just fair and green
    Were now gray and torn;
And the folks were the saddest folk, I ween,
    That e'er were born.

They could not dance—they could not sing—
And no more they went a-merrying,
For a shadow fell o'er everything
    From hill to strand,
And the angel of woe spread out his wing
    Over all the land.

Then I said to the angel, "Read to me
This riddle or this mystery.
What are these awful things I see;
    These scenes explain,
These portents, or what they may be,
    Which craze my brain."

The angel answered not; but in
A twinkling stirred Manassas' din,
And in the background, "Thus we win,"
    Was writ, and near
Was, "Oh, my country," as its twin,
    Engraven clear.

Quicker than thought before me spread
Another scene; 'twas Shiloh red
With gore, and Sidney Johnston dead;
    And as before
'Twas, "Oh, my country," at his head,
    Engraved in gore.

Quicker than thought, than flash of light,
The scene at Fred'ricksburg, the night
At Chancellor's—oh, the mad'ning sight,
    Stonewall lay slain;
And "Oh, my country," graved in white,
    Made his vict'ry vain.

Quicker than thought, in awful guise
And heralded by moans and cries,
The valley and the hill of sighs
    Ensanguined pass—
Pale Gettysburg flared in my eyes,
    And Bull Run the last.

And Chickamauga's rage and wrath,
Dyeing with blood, a twelve mile path;
And Mission Ridge, her aftermath
    Of streams of gore,
Round Chattanooga death's wide swath,
    Spreads my eyes before.

The Wilderness, witch-haunted land,
Where armies struggled hand to hand
And fury ev'ry passion fanned;
    Cold Harbor taking,
Her hot bath, fierce before me stand,
    Spectral moan making.

Resaca and Atlanta red
With blood by none but heroes shed,
A horrid panorama spread,
    And central writ
Was "Oh, my country "—"oh, my dead!"
    Emblazoning it.

Thus, "Oh, my country," was the wail,
The legend, in each battle's trail,
On the conquered or the victor's mail;
    The chorus sad
To ev'ry pæan, ev'ry "hail,"
    Those struggles had.

The Presence spoke not yet, but lest
The riddle dark should go unguessed,
He pointed calmly to the west—
    To Franklin's height,
The wildest, darkest, bitterest,
    Closing at night.

——8

And I see athwart this scene, again
Writ as if written with a pen,
Just over Cleburne and his men
        Piled deep in death :
" Victory but death—thus, thus we win,"
        Freedom's Shibboleth.

Thus in my dream so wildly true,
A dream within a dream I knew,
While mem'ry made a sharp review
        Of prospects vast,
In which had been some dark ado,
        From first to last.

Bull Run to Franklin, each confessed,
Vict'ry was death; so with the rest,
And my inner dream said it was best,
        As time would show,
To have made this sacrificial test
        For weal or woe.

Thus scene on scene of horror passed
Before me as I looked aghast,
Victorious fields but carnage vast,
        And underneath
Was " Oh, my country," first and last—
        Victory but death.

" Now hide your face," the angel said,
" And let this last scene pass.   The dead
Have shut the door of Janus dread,
    And both are free—
Master and servant by bloodshed—
    So mote it be.

" Yes, hide your face," the angel said,
" And bow your head, and bow your head,
Over the dead—the sacred dead—
    Over the tomb,
Where trail the red, the white and the red :
    Their end has come."

And while I mourned, and mourned, and mourned,
And my heart and brain with anguish burned,
And while above that tomb I yearned
    Disconsolate,
And youth's sweet tide to Mara turned—
    And love to hate—

Again the solemn Presence spoke :
" Arise, arise--awake, awake—
Still battle for your country's sake,
    To rebuild her fanes ;
The shackles from her limbs to break
    To you remains.

" To fill her garners and her stalls,
To build her fences and her walls,
To hearken to her plaintive calls,
    While yet she pines;
To guide her while she stumbling falls,
    To rear her shrines.

" To rock her precious cradles, and
To take her children by the hand,
And teach them how to walk and stand
    As heroes do,
And to love their land, their smitten land,
    Like patriots true.

" To cherish with regard devout
Her women's virtue, and about
Her shrines (dishonor still kept out)
    To rear a fence
Of valiant trust, and a redoubt
    Of reverence.

" To help her poor ones in their need,
And through their night their steps to lead;
To bind their wounds up when they bleed—
    To fight their fight,
And in their homes to sow the seed
    Of doing right.

"To plead the cause of justice—ay,
To hold her banner firm and high;
To rear her church spires tow'rds the sky,
        And to keep those aisles
Clean as Eden's were, when Eve's soft eye
        Taught Adam smiles.

"To work, not weep; to stir, not mope;
To wrestle with the Angel Hope,
And turn not loose unblessed: to cope
        With inner foes,
And help to widen labor's scope
        And not its woes.

"To learn a mastery, like divine—
Not over others, as of swine—
But the mastery of self: in fine
        To keep the peace;
To keep what is yours and give me mine,
        And war will cease."

And then the wild'ring spell was broke,
And from my wond'rous dream I woke,
But what the presence did and spoke,
        Can I forget?
For it smote me like a lightning stroke,
        And it smites me yet.

AT MY OFFICE WINDOW.

Who is that, papa?   A beggar, my boy,
Just sent for a season the rich to annoy;
Not wanting in brains, and not wanting in wit,
Nor wanting in energy, "never a bit."
But wanting in principle, honor and truth,
And the maker of lies from his earliest youth :
Beware how a lie, ev'n in jest, you would tell—
There's nothing so damnable this side of hell.

And what is that, papa?   A teacher, my child.
He's a safe middle man, neither praised nor reviled;
He is going, he fancies, to win him a name,
And maybe a dollar or so with his fame.
But he dreams but a dream, whether foolish or not,
That keeps him still blind to his real hard lot;
His profession's too big for a mortal to bear,
But he never was known to be killed by despair.
And here is the secret, my sweet little man—
He shuffles it off just as soon as he can.
Oh, the sight of a dead "live teacher" is rare !

What is that, papa?   A sycophant, child,
Who worships a thing like himself : is beguiled
By the gaudy exterior of power : and licks
His hand like a dog, like a dog takes his kicks.
He's a numerous people out there in the street,
And fellows like him on each corner you meet ;
Their self is so altered by swapping around,
Has belonged to so many, 'tis only a sound
That differ's in ev'ry one's mouth ; it is nought
In the battle of action—the struggle of thought :
A disciple of virtue, from vices exempt,
Yet being a toady the heir of contempt.

What is that, papa ?   A fraud, my son ;
He shines in the crown another has won,
He snickers, and dickers, and bows all galore,
But his kiss is a stab, and he stabs to the core.
The dream of his life is an ultimate trick,
The straight beaten pathway of truth makes him sick.
You may know him in church, you may see him in
    state,
The dunce is his prey and the fool is his bait
To catch bigger fish with ; so watch him, my son,
When sweetest he's deadliest—please him, but shun.

What is that, papa?   A fool, my boy,
With a head full of brains and a heart full of joy,

But he stops not to think, and he can't understand,
That the world's not a play-ground or sweet fairy
    land,
But a storm-beaten shore, or a rude field of briars,
With its valleys of floods and its mountains of fires;
Where none but the toilers and sweaters are fit
To the seats of the worthy to clamber and sit.
That fellow goes flinging his talents away,
And the night time will catch him asleep or at play.

What is that, papa?   A scribbler, my man;
He is getting the news just as fast as he can.
Don't you see how he writes, how he rattles along,
So " rough at a venter " with pencil and tongue.
All he wants is a dot--jusl a shadow of fact—
He trims it and spreads it with cunning exact,
And it grows like a vine, but it changes, alas!
Till the fact is no longer the fact that it was.
His energy copy, his skill emulate--
But facts, with the utmost precision, relate.

What is that, papa?   A drunkard, my child;
I knew him long since in the far away wild,
He was up on the hill, I was down in the vale—
He at Luxury's head, I at Poverty's tail.
His ways were so sweet and his voice to my ear
Seemed ever melodious, charming to hear.

And the way he could tell you his feeling or
    thought,
A smile or a tear irresistibly brought.
He was sturdy and strong—he was steady and true,
He was generous, gallant and gentle as you;
And a tenderer heart and a merrier man
When he met at a frolic ne'er shuffled in bran.
Now he follows his demon, as led by the arm,
For oh, he is changed both in spirit, mind, form.
He is up and he's down, like the grass of the plain,
The play of the wind both in temper and brain;
With a purposeless motion, unsteady he goes,
Led by what he now fancies and not what he knows.
Though coquetting with fortune she still hovers
    near,
And will not desert him, she holds him so dear.

What is that, papa?   An editor, sir,
A man like the witch with a caldron to stir;
And stir it he does with a feverish brain
And a quivering nerve, till the syllables rain
From the tip of his wand—to befuddle the folk
With his strong necromancy as stifling as smoke;
Yet hot as the fire and persuasive as light,
Which softens the wrong till it looks like the right.
Yet a sentry is he on the farthest outpost;

Where the danger is greatest, the storm threatens
    most,
He signals the people, by night and by day,
With his white flag of truce or his red flag for fray.
And he sounds on his bugle, when peace calls us home,
The honeyed strain of the bee in the comb.
But the gold, or the beautiful fame which he seeks,
He finds not, except in the rosier cheeks
Of his dear mother land; for a toiler is he,
Who gathers his sweets, like the poor honey bee,
For others to eat; his fruition he sees
O'er the River in rest 'neath the shade of the trees.

What is that, papa?   A miser, my lad.
He is searching for something the world never had,
That is happiness wrapped in a kerchief of gold;
Or enthroned in a palace of treasure untold,
He's afraid of his shadow which walks by his side,
When candle in hand his sweet money he'd hide.
He's ragged and hungry; he's selfish and vile;
And naught but a dollar can waken his smile.
Yet, darling, he once was as lovely as you.
And he saw heav'nly visions as boys only do;
But he built him an idol—an idol of gold—
And there paid his life vows; the sequel behold.
Now what are the beauties of nature to him,

Idolatry flings o'er the spirit a film ;
And where is the magic of woman's bright eye,
And where the enchantment of love's soft reply,
And where is the charm of the tulip or rose,
To quicken his joys, or deaden his woes.

What is that, papa ?   A thing, my boy :
He once was like you, dear, his mother's joy ;
But now he is loose from her apron string,
And he sports a garotte and he flashes a ring,
And he smokes cigarettes and he ogles the girls,
And sometimes he nurses his own dainty curls.
And I know what I've seen, that he giggles in church,
And the reason of this is the lack of a " birch."
Let him pass, if he lives, (and I reckon he will,
Death loves not the mark where's there's little to kill),
Thro' this chrysalis state, and this torpor of mind,
He may yet be a man to be toasted and dined.

What is that, papa ? A dude, my child.
By the love of himself he is fondly beguiled ;
He looks rather frail to be going about,
Yet his lady, brave girl, well knows he is out.
She ventures with him to the german, you know,
And supports him while shaking the 'wildering toe.
Let him pass ; for the country is safe, you may say,
When his sort have to keep the invader away.

What is that, papa?   A farmer, my son.
He's a man, though he looks like the " son-of-a-gun."
He lives, as he ought, in the sweat of his face,
And nothing is sadder to him than disgrace.
Don't think him a fool; there is little in looks :
He's not witless because he's behind in his books.
He reads from a book that is better and greater
Than your's—its author, the Perfect Creator;
His walk is with nature from morning till night,
And whatever he learns from her teaching is right.
She speaks to him daily with mystical tongues,
She sings to him nightly her mystical songs ;
In slumber the sweetest she laps him at night,
And wakes him each morn by the kiss of her light :
She gives to his nostrils the sweetest of breath,
From the flowers that blossom and sigh on the heath ;
Being nearest to her in her beautiful breast,
She gives him Elysian dreams and rest.

YESTERDAY AND TODAY.

In the land of the South there were voices of moan,
Like the sounds round our cabins when winter has
    blown,
All the lutes and guitars—all the silvery bells—
Were hushed in the halls and unheard in the dells.

For the stateliest flowers that grew by the way
To the besom of war they had fallen a prey;
And the vigor, the pride, and the beauty once ours
Were swept from the land like the leaves from the
    bowers. .

Lo, the might of our valleys was wasted in war,
And the light of our homes seemed to glimmer afar,
And the spirit of joy, like a beauty in shroud,
Or the sun in a mist, only flashed through a cloud.

All the people glanced back o'er the war darkened
    past,
With a mem'ry of tears for their glories o'ercast;

And their songs were but dirges o'er hopes that were
    dead,
Like the sighs of the bowers when summer is fled.

The eyes of the people, if turned to the west,
Saw battlements crowned with the enemy's crest,
And the eyes of the people, if turned to the east,
Saw their hordes, like a vulture, swoop down to the
    feast.

Tow'rds the North, East and West, tow'rds our own
    Mexic' main,
Rose the plea of the people for peace, but in vain ;
So a murmur of madness swept over the land,
Like the froth of the breakers which war 'gainst the
    strand.

For the friends of the past grew deceitful and cold,
The cause of the righteous none rose to uphold,
And we sat down in ashes, heart broken and wild,
But looking up, Hagar-like—lo! heaven smiled.

And a new song was put in our mouths as we sighed—
A song of rebuke to the nations of pride,
A song of the folk who had bowed to the rod,
A song of the folk who had trusted in God.

Like the wails of the winter winds dying away,
When the sweet South sighs soft as a herald of May,
One by one went our wails when our fetters were
    broke,
And hope lit her stars in the breast of the folk.

Soon the murmur was heard in the valley no more,
New flowers sprung sweet on the hill and the shore,
And fingers of beauty grew cunning to weave
The garment, the mantle, the bonnet, the sleeve.

New fires on the altars of liberty blazed,
New cities of refuge like magic were raised,
New carols were sung in savannah and wold,
And the people each other began to uphold.

And the people drew nearer together again—
Drew nearer together in pleasure and pain—
And met, as of yore, at the altar to pray,
And vows hymeneal to pledge day by day.

So the sweet birds of music, of pleasure, of mirth,
As our skies grew the brighter came back to our earth,
For the folk on each other and God made their call,
And closer united, stood firm as a wall.

Now a new song we hear in the whirring of mills,
And a new song we hear in the shafts of the hills,

And a new song we hear in the merry play grounds,
As the teacher, the prophet of peace, makes his
    rounds.

And a new song is heard up the iron-ribbed vale,
As the horse with his nostrils of fire takes his trail,
Through darkness, through tunnel, his journey is
    sped,
With a hoarse incantation he forges ahead.

Yet mem'ry will hang round the shrines of the past,
Where glory and honor kept tryst to the last,
And the hearts of the old folk, though thoughtful and
    wise,
Cannot wholly repress mem'ry's tears from the eyes.

That mem'ry 's parcel and part of their lives,
Like the sons of their loins and that mem'ry survives,
And the dreams that they dream, and the works that
    they do,
To the old time are wedded, and not to the new.

'Tis the youth of the land that were cradled in woe,
That must waken and stir—must victorious go—
'Tis the youth of the land that must take up the song,
And all of its valorous murmurs prolong.

If the song be of progress, 'tis theirs in a choir
To fill its new measures with chivalry's fire,
To temper the strength of the day, and the brawn,
With the mellow sweet grace of the day that is gone.

If the song be of might or dominion, 'tis theirs
To sing what the oracle only declares—
To tread no false measure, to sing no false strains,
To remember the truth, though remembered in chains.

If the song be of building, teach well to the choirs
The song of foundations ere that of the spires,
That the children of each farthest people may know,
When the turrets are high they have granite below.

That the children may sing from their own happy
    hearts
Life's song in its several beautiful parts,
And catching from habit the spirit of song
Together harmonious through life press along.

This sweet consummation of things I behold,
As I see a clear dawn in a twilight of gold ;
The people, our oracles, show it to me—
And God's with the people, and so it must be.

—— 9

THE RAGGED VOLUNTEER.

I stood a sentry 'mongst the hills
    Where gushed the haunted fountains,
And leaped the torrents, splashed the rills,
    In weird Smoky Mountains.
I saw no cabin door, I heard
        No crow of chanticleer,
    But on a slab a little bird
    Sat piping, and my lone watch cheered;
    And cut upon a slab appeared
        This token of remembrance dear:
        " The ragged volunteer."

Longstreet and Burnside here had been
    In bristling fierce array,
Georgia and old Kentucky's men—
    The angry blue and gray,
Dear Alabama's bugle blew
        Beside yon fountain clear.
Sure some of all these soldier's knew

A hero faithful, still and true,
Who bid his comrades here adieu.
One deemed it epitaph enough
To scratch upon this slab so rough
    This token of remembrance dear :
    " The ragged volunteer."

Ah, those who followed, true and tried,
  Longstreet, the old war horse,
Who famine, sickness, death defied,
  For better or for worse ;
With him and Buckner and his men,
Who fought in this big slaughter pen,
    Saw as a sad familiar sight
      Our noblest and most dear.
Our bluest bloods—our white most white—
Cheerful and brave in rags bedight,
In camp, on march, or in the fight,
Saw men with names at home go down
Without a single glory crown—
And ne'er be seen or heard of more,
Along time's raven haunted shore,
    Whose epitaph is like this here :
    " The ragged volunteer."

Their long neglected slabs are found
  By dark Potomac's wave,

And over many a noble mound
  The moaning pine trees wave,
By rough Stone River many lie
      O'er whom no slabs appear,
    And where the James flows sluggish by,
    Unknown is written far and nigh ;
    And over all, with truthful pen,
    We write to-day—one of our men :
      " A ragged volunteer."

Shoeless, and jacketless, some went,
  Those poor brave boys in gray,
With ragged blanket and no tent
  Thro' winter's night they lay.
Hard time's its terrors lost, and death
      Itself, so often near,
    Lost all his grimness. His was faith,
    Entitled to a fadeless wreath,
    And with the Father, let us trust
    A mansion for the saintly just
Will be given him who trusted here :
      " The ragged volunteer."

IN MEMORIAM.

[Poem read before the "Confederate Veterans' Association"
on Memorial Day—April 26th, 1891.]

But yesterday it seems to me
We furled the banner over Lee:
But yesterday the stars and bars
Were taken from the hands of Mars:
But yesterday the men in gray,
Like troubadours came homeward gay—
No vengeance finding lodgment in
Those hearts, whose legend still had been
And was, howe'er their die was cast,
My home—my southland first and last.
No bitter memories and no hate,
No mourning o'er a cruel fate,
They came with cheer from North to South
Still with a new song in their mouth,
To find the fire fiend on their hills,
The shattered turbines of their mills,

Their cabins desolate, and their barns
Begirt and hid in briary tarns,
And yet they were so glad to see
The sweet charms of the used to be,
The olden haunts—the mother there,
Smit as she was with more than care;
Perchance a noble father too,
To clasp them as they used to do:
So glad to kiss their sister's cheek,
And e'en "old mammy's" roof to seek.
So glad to wander round the place;
Tho' it wore an unfamiliar face,
To see what olden charms remained,
What olden glory home retained.
So glad to stretch in peaceful shade,
Where brook or bird sweet music made;
So glad to hear the bee's soft hum
And not the 'larum of the drum;
To list the silvery waters pour,
And not the opening battle's roar;
So glad to lay them in their beds
Without a rifle at their heads,
Without the picket on the hill
Or sentry station by the rill;
So glad to roll upon the sward,
Nor meet a sergeant of the guard;

So glad in sheltered walls again
To hide from sleet and snow and rain;
So glad to hear no whirring shot
From mountain gorge or woody spot;
So glad to be aroused no more
By picket firing—cannon roar;
They had no heart for bitterness;
They had no lips to curse, but bless;
They had no time to think of hate,
Nor to complain of cruel fate;
Nor yet to mourn the backward scene,
Once bright with hope and glory's sheen.
Their minds seemed shut against regret,
Their footsteps all were forward set;
Accustomed long to faces front,
To fortify against the brunt,
To charge obedient to command
Or 'mid a storm of shot to stand;
To move not either left or right,
To make and not direct the fight;
But hearing orders not to pause
To criticize or ask the cause,
But up to victory's heights to lay
Their bleeding forms to pave the way.
They grew up, as it were to be
Above the servile hireling; free

From those base instincts which men show
When disaster dark or overthrow
Confronts—free from that vileness shown
By those who think of self alone,
So they had into Bayards grown ;
Without reproach or fear—full high
Above the average height of such
As dare not for their country die,
When true men meet in deadly clutch,
They walked upon the lofty plane
Of such as wear but duty's chain.
Yet with them went and with them came
The comrades of the past the same ;
Whether in sturdy presence near,
Whether to mem'ry only dear :
For unforgotten were the dead,
Who by them in the ditch had bled ;
Who fought at Gettysburg with them—
There won the martyr's diadem,
Or by the Rappahannock's wave
Went down into an unknown grave ;
Stood true at Donelson, and died
Where ev'ry woe the soldier tried
At Franklin, Shiloh, Perryville ;
At fierce Cold Harbor faithful still,
In each and ev'ry trial stood,

Upon the land, upon the flood,
The direst tests that man could stand,
In love of home and native land.
These ever present—unforgot
Came to the mansion and the cot
From out their spirit land, and wrought
A magnanimity of thought
In those surviving them and strife,
And whispered them of nobler life,
And kept them as by mystic spell
Bound to a valorous principle.
And 'tis our grateful memory now
We gather meekly to avow
Their valor—to recount and own
That half the glory we have known,
And half the power that we claim
Has been reflected by their name.
In yonder city of the dead
There may not be one narrow bed
In which a Southern soldier sleeps,
O'er which an aged mother weeps
Disconsolate—for years, long years
Which seals the fountain of our tears
Has failed to wash his image out—
There may not rest one gallant scout
Who died in grapple with the foe

At Chickamauga long ago,
Or closed with Stonewall all his wars
At weird Melzie Chancellor's,
Or bathed the slopes of Malvern Hill
With blood which kings might weep to spill;
It was such royal, taintless blood,
Unsullied as Castalia's flood.
There may not rest one hardy tar
That got on sea his latest scar,
Beneath the sod of yon fair hill,
But for their mem'ries sacred still
We'll twine our wreaths and lay them there,
And bid the fairies of the air
Go take our mem'ries thus expressed,
O'er valley wide—o'er mountain crest,
To each and every far off grot,
To each and ev'ry sacred spot
Which keeps—is honored with the keeping—
The bones o'er which we still are weeping.
Yes, take these mem'ries sweet of ours,
And strew them as we strew these flowers,
And leave the precious freight with them
As a memorial diadem.
Tomorrow morn the flowers will fade,
Scarce leave their odors in the glade,
But what their wreathing signifies

Will live as long as Paradise.
Wherever love of country finds
A lodgment in the people's minds,
This burning sentiment, this strong
Remembrance shall inspire the song.
The history of the people and
The patriotism of all the land
From Tampa to Sault St. Marie,
From Champlain to the Mexic' sea,
And our proud children of after years
Will mingle praises, smiles and tears,
And scarcely learn—nor wish to know
Which was the friend, which was the foe.

What have been problems intricate
For long, long years, by dint of hate,
More tangled grown—not by the sword
Of warrior or the ballot horde,
Not by the statesman's pen or tongue,
Not by the poet's burning song
Resolved ; not by the school of trade
Where mutual interests are made,
Not solved by teacher, prelate, priest ;
But when all cunning plans have ceased,
They'll yet be solvod above the graves
Of Southern and of Northern braves,

Who fought for principle and died
In duty's harness glorified.
And after while the hardy boy
Of far Astoria, whose chief joy
Is breasting winter's ice and snows,
And conquering obstacles with blows,
Will by his clear, cold Willamette,
His red cheeks towards the South's wind set,
To kneel him at the fragrant shrine
Of one whose rose and columbine
Round winter's neck hang clustering still,
His lap with od'rous flowers to fill,
And Florida and Oregon
Will kiss each other and be one,
And the sweet dreams from off the seas
Of our own shining Cyclades,
With gentle lapses, wooings strange,
Working as 'twere a chymic change,
Will fire the thought of colder climes
And smooth the front of harder times,
And from this kiss of sun and snow
The happy wave of peace will flow,
And 'twill be current on each breeze
From Northern lakes or Southern seas;
These children love each other true,
Their fathers love each other, too;

These sacred mounds contain the fires
Of noble, patriotic sires,
Who taught all other people's this :—
There is no vain self-sacrifice,
That blood heroic wins acclaim,
No matter what its fountain's name.

Land of the South, where the storm cloud of war.
Gathering fury from near and afar,
Hurtled it bolts of destruction so long
Till every valley to anguish was wrung,
Till every town had a ghost in its hall
And every fountain its wormwood and gall,
And every bower its adder to dread
And every high couch its sword overhead,
Lift up your face, for the tempest is gone ;
Over the hills comes the radiant dawn,
Out of the womb of the grief-stricken past
Vict'ry and triumph and peace come at last.
Snatched from your head is the thorn crown you wore,
Clean is your scutcheon, and swept is your floor.
Out of the ashes of sons that have bled,
That they might quiet your sorrow and dread,
That they might answer your call of alarm,
That they might shield you from insult and harm :
Out of these ashes great mem'ries are born ;

Memories, the bitterest foe, cannot scorn.
Cherish them, nurse them with motherly care,
Keep them as oracles sacred and rare,
Keep them as landmarks of other sad years,
Keep them for history's triumphant tears.

Oh, land of the South with your royal traditions,
 How green are the laurels entwining your brow
And green will they be, while these sacred possessions
 These graves of your heroes are tended as now,
While our sons and our daughters forget not the sires,
Chief priests of those altars, where freedom respires.

Ev'ry wreath that your sons in their day have en-
 twined them,
 But adds a new grace to the heart and the hand,
Which quicken their mem'ries and tenderly bind them
 In bright immortelles for the shrines of the land,
Their symbols and purpose we cannot repress,
Neglected they curse, and regarded they bless.

For those mem'ries must live—like the cedar must
 flourish,
 Or the glory and pride of the people will fly.
A people ashamed of their history should perish,
 And a people ashamed of their heroes must die,
For what is a land with no history—no braves,
The despised of the world and the mother of slaves.

How blest then the people whose graves are remem-
    bered,
  Who nurse with devotion the memory of all
Whose names with Thermopylæ's few may be num-
    bered,
  As immortal far less in their rise than their fall,
For thousands have triumphed, yet who knows their
    name?
But Leonidas falling won fame, deathless fame.

Our past I regret not, tho' solemn its story,
  'Twas begun, and continued, and closed in mishap.
The result may be likened to winter all hoary,
  Forerunner of spring with the rose in its lap,
For the winter of war times is past, and the spring
With its turtle of peace over all spreads her wing.

Ah, had not these dead whom we cover with roses,
  Like heroes each fortune unselfishly met,
These spots, where each sleeper in honor reposes,
  Were deprived of a mention few sepulchres get,
And the lesson their passionate sacrifice taught,
Not glory, but shame, to the people had brought.

But their fate unconsidered, with nothing but duty
  To guide them through sorrow, through carnage
    untold,

They rose to the heights of the city of beauty,
  And their names in the book of the true are enrolled,
And their record down here we shall read, mark and
      learn,
And be proud of the ashes that lie in each urn.

And such urns are the caskets of jewels resplendent,
  Whose flash cannot long undiscovered remain,
While remembrance, their vesta and faithful attendant,
  Keeps stirring them still with an ecstatic pain,
To catch from their glances some spark of that flame
Which kindles the lamps in our temple of fame.

These graves are, methinks, but the sacred high places,
  Whence the muse of our history will loudly proclaim
To the children of children our worth and our praises,
  Or else from the record we give her—our shame.
In guarding these places, our pride we declare—
In neglecting we say, lo! our traitors lie there.

Sure, these sleepers hold title to long recollection,
  To rev'rent report of their struggle and fate,
Their valor and principle gave them direction,
  The plaudits of comrades their shades now await;
When their story we tell to the world, as it is,
We but render to Cæsar the things that are his.

This rev'rent report at their graves we are making:
    We make it in flowers and banners still furled,
Ere long from the bondage of prejudice breaking,
    'Twill be writ by the muse in the heart of the world,
When the watchword will be to the grand round of
        braves,
    " American citizens sleep in these graves."

Let us bide, then, our season's arrival, in patience;
    Like a ship from the billows and storms it will come;
And healing will drip from its sails, for the nations—
    The bright sister nations, whose radiant sum
May be counted in stars in our banner unfurled,
Where those stars blaze together, the joy of the world.

EPISTLE TO SUE.

NO. I.

I haven't forgot to remember
  I promised to write you a verse
  When you left us, dear girl, in September,
Some notions of mine to rehearse.

Perchance, as my sentences jingle,
  Some curious things I may say,
When the pleasant and better I mingle,
  And mercurial temper betray.

First of all, I'll begin with the former,
  As the idea pops in my head,
To pledge you I think you a charmer,
  Accomplished, and very well bred.

Educated all round, 'tis no wonder
  In witcheries sweet you are versed,
Notwithstanding you cause us to ponder
  O'er crotchets by which you are cursed.

I must own, though—don't blush—you are pretty ;
    But " beauty is only skin deep,"
And a dozen as fair in the city
    Are held in my eyes very cheap.

For beauty, in fact, unattended
    By graces of heart and of mind,
Hasn't much, after all, to commend it,
    In itself, being only enshrined.

I can say, in this pleasant connection,
    I think both these graces are yours,
And I trust it may prove a conviction
    When I catch you some day doing chores.

For a woman is ne'er so enchanting
    As when she has learned to forget,
That cheap little crow of self-vaunting,
    When she plays at the head of her " set."

When instead of becoming imperious,
    Exacting and cross, she should be
More gentle, more modest and serious,
    And from tricks of effrontery free.

Now the bachelors—horrid old fellows—
    Observe all her pranks with a sneer,

And think ev'ry soul of them jealous,
    And querulous, envious and queer.

'Tis well to avoid such aspersion,
    By rememb'ring that beauty has foes,
Who make their especial diversion
    To hunt for the rents in your clothes.

Right here, as germane to the subject,
    Let's talk of these bachelors queer,
And a lesson we'll teach through the object —
    The best way of teaching, my dear.

To their claim to a special gentility,
    That depends—but we make no comment:
To their claim to a special virility,
    We argument join with dissent.

Their title to wisdom's a fiction :
    'Tis really funny and queer,
In the *spell* lies a sad contradiction—
    They are *sere* but they cannot be *seer*

A selfish, unnatural living
    Begets an unnatural way
Of thinking, and even believing,
    And makes them another's bewray.

They are surely a genus peculiar,
  Who never their dreams overtake,
Though truthful withal, they must fool you,
  If only for oddity's sake.

They seldom are men whose digestion
  Can vie with the ostrich or crane,
So comfort is out of the question—
  They are therefore, in one sense, insane.

Their brains and their bowels together
  Seem wedded and close intertwined,
More dependent the one on the other,
  Than those of the rest of mankind.

Their bowels and brains of compassion,
  In sickness are one and the same:
And in health—this is out of the fashion—
  They differ in nothing but name.

In truth it is truly pathetic
  To consider their ailments and pains,
And nought but a mighty emetic
  Can sever their bowels and brains.

The one has a pet of a notion,
  The other a misery to pet;

Both are held with a kind of devotion—
    Both are lost with a kind of regret.

Thus has it been often contended
    That love in the bowels began,
Held the heart for a while, then ascended,
    And died in the head of the man.

Methinks 'tis not so with the woman :
    In her brain, I believe, it was set,
Whence it creeps to her bowels, and no man
    Ere saw where it died in her yet.

With the bachelor, though, so contrary,
    A different judgment applies—
Opinions and theories vary,
    For still at a tangent he flies.

For as time in his case slow unravels
    The knotty old skein of his life,
Love stops in his heart, from his travels
    Up and down, when this man gets a wife.

Now talking of love and the sexes,
    He seems to reserve for the cranks
All his lotions and charms, which he mixes
    And doses them with, in his pranks.

And wholly set free from delusion,
  Maids and baches are both at a loss—
Are thrown into gloomy confusion,
  And prefer for a change to be cross.

A blind man can see what's the matter
  With humorous people like these,
Though laughing and growing the fatter,
  They're losing their hope by degrees.

For little by little, the vigor
  And glory of life fades and dies,
Till their hope, once a sun, gets no bigger
  Than a faint little star in the skies.

No matter how fluent and sparkling,
  Their language may be, 'tis in vain :
A growing depression comes darkling,
  And binds them as strong as a chain.

They cease to be zealous and clannish,
  They dream of themselves more and more,
And bitter reflections still banish
  The happy delusions of yore.

But such, of St. Paul are commended ;
  He saw all the world at a glance,
Or he ne'er would have writ as he then did,
  On a theme so replete with romance.

EPISTLE TO S. I. R.

NO. II.

Dear Sue, 'twas an excellent letter
  You wrote with your cunning white hand,
And I tell you sincerely a better
  A fellow could scarcely demand.

But I thought it the least bit disjointed,
  And the least bit sarcastic may be :
In my letter you seemed disappointed,
  Though your page didn't say so to me.

Yet I thought I could read in your scribble
  Far more than was written in words ;
But I saw through your beautiful quibble,
  As I see through the carol of birds.

Now you know when their song is the gladdest,
  There's a strain now and then of complaint,
And the merriest blends with the saddest,
  'Till at best 'tis an amorous feint.

This conceit may awaken a bubble
  Of dissent and a merry pooh, pooh !
But I argue without any trouble
  I can show you my witness is true.

Truth's best pioneer is fancy,
  In hypothesis science begins,
And the devil's trump card—necromancy,
  For ages that kuklux of sins—

Has become, in the light of researches,
  Religion herself in the van,
The strength of the states and the churches—
  An evangel of blessings to man.

The high muck-a-muck of all fancies,
  The people are fighting today,
Is this talk with the dead in seances,
  Where spirits heaven's secrets betray.

This electra will prove, as I take it,
  Another evangel heav'n blest,
When the shell that enwombs her we break it,
  And put her to work with the rest.

I therefore make bold to acknowledge
  Mind reading an art, not a wile;

From the gates of the psychical college
    It will pass to the church afterwhile.

Mind reading I oft have attempted
    For the curious love of the thing,
No science from search have exempted
    That touches the slave and the king.

Their writings—their sayings—their doings,
    Their gestures—their manners—their looks—
Their schemings—their hatings and wooings,
    Their lives in and out of the books.

Each and all are but pilots to guide us
    To their mystical caverns below,
To the springs of their lives long denied us
    Which time and occasion but show.

These secrets come up in our writings,
    And the springs of our actions declare,
And our mystical selves and soul-fightings
    To the eyes of the blind man lay bare.

Mind reading, I thus have essayed it,
    Your secret emotions to scan,
And I've thought while your letter I read it,
    That its deep undercurrent thus ran:

"You wrote not a word of the 'wimmen'
  Who thought I was mean to the core,
And you said not a word of the 'gemmen'
  Who so gallantly haunted my door.

"Of the smart and chivalric Canadian,
  Who escorted me oft to the lake,
And called me a lily of Aidin,
  You said not a word for my sake.

"Of Richard, the tall and the 'sassy,'
  Of 'Daniel O'Rucker,' the smart,
Of George, the conceited and gassy,
  And of Lev, that was nearest my heart.

"You made in your letter no mention ;
  But scolded and scolded away,
And showed very plain your intention
  To lash me for being so gay.

"I notice such things, I assure you :
  For what do I care for a verse
That says not, 'my dear, I adore you.'
  Or does not my praises rehearse.

"And what do I care for your chatter
  If it hints not of people I love,

Or of those loving me—but no matter,
    Your letter I did not approve."

Thus I read it—I may be mistaken—
    But you " had orter thought it," I know;
And I'm certain you gave me a rakin';
    But love-licks back at you I'll throw.

For, darling, I know I intended
    To write what you wanted to hear,
But thought first of all, " I'll be candid,"
    Then pleasant and newsy, my, dear.

I felt it would always be pleasant
    To chat of the gallants down here,
Who tell me, though absent, you're present—
    And they swear it is so—but it's queer.

Any time, then, I fancy, will answer,
    To waft you their memories sweet,
In the shape of a rhyme or a stanza,
    Or in prose, if 'tis polished and neat.

I'm afraid, though—don't say I am snarling—
    They prize your *vivacity* most,
'Tis the fly and the candle, my darling,
    And the moral—a chapter on *toast*.

If your heart be the thing they are after,
　No cynic on earth could object,
But this hunting for giggles and laughter
　We endure, but we cannot affect.

And one thing I tell you for certain,
　I am sure you will own it half true,
Men come now too often a-flirtin'—
　Too seldom heart-broken to woo.

Sometimes this depends on the weather—
　The weather does wonderful things—
Sometimes on the father and mother,
　Who clip off the young gallants' wings.

Sometimes beaux await an occasion,
　Well suited their woes to rehearse;
Sometimes they are speechless with passion,
　Most times they are *empty of purse.*

All this on the man is a damper,
　And keeps him from bending the knee,
'Till youth's opportunities scamper
　And leave but the sad used-to-be.

Alas, for the lamps that keep burning
　From night unto night all the same;

Alas, for the hearts which keep yearning
    To catch just a glimpse of love's flame.

They chat of another's romances—
    Of the hero and heroine's cares—
But themselves keep away from love's trances,
    And never make mention of theirs.

Thus the beautiful belles of the city,
    Who claim such a bevy of beaux,
While with them are merry and witty,
    But without them are almost morose.

Now the girls of the village don't do so;
    They play with their gallants awhile,
Then they hint of a ring or a trousseau,
    Or treat them with manners *horsestyle*.

Now a fellow well kicked, you should know it,
    Comes down very soon to his knees,
And his passion he's certain to show it—
    That's the end to attain, if you please.

And yet, if you don't care a nickel
    Whether fellows come wooing or not,
But believe you would be in a pickle
    With anyone sharing your lot :

Perhaps it is better to giggle—
　To simper and smirk to the end ;
And trust after all to inveigle
　Some gump into being a friend.

For toothless old maids can be frisky,
　And gush as the pretty girls do,
Can avoid married life—that's so risky,
　And sometimes so terrible, too.

They can fix up their neighborhood matches,
　The trousseaus and weddings arrange,
And for many torn hearts furnish patches,
　But for theirs get no patch for a change.

They can giggle and simper till fifty,
　And the glamour of youth so affect,
And in dress a la mode be so shifty,
　As to fool even fashion's elect.

They can counterfeit roses so neatly
　That nature, deceived going by,
Commends them for acting so sweetly,
　And leaves them another supply.

But their necks will get yellow and stringy,
　While their brows show the footprints of time,

And their walk, once so graceful and springy,
    Will appear on a level to climb.

And the halls where with young hopes they sported
    With bright dreams ran many a race,
When they've vanished, will seem all deserted,
    And no fairies can fill up their place.

All in all, 'tis a sorrowful picture,
    But I throw not a tuft or a stone,
I make not a comment or stricture
    On their motives for living alone.

But I never consent to abuse 'em
    Except for the lives they have crossed.
I am sorry that men have to lose 'em
    And know not the glory they've lost.

Ne'ertheless, I believe, it is better
    To fall into line with crowd ·
To gracefully yield to the fetter
    Which makes all of womanhood proud.

To take all the risks and the chances
    In the battle of true womanhood—
Its anguish, its follies, its trances—
    For such are evangels of good.

Thus write I a curious letter,
  For the subject discussed, though so old,
Like wine gets with age, all the better,
  And like snowballs, the larger when rolled.

Perhaps if again you should read it,
  A reason as well as a rhyme
May oracular rise, when you need it,
  Don't burn this, sweet girl, till that time.

EPISTLE TO SUE.

NO. III.

The little you wrote me was only
   A little, as measured by words;
But finding a fellow, when lonely
   And bothered, was sweeter than birds.

To me it was chuck full of matter,
   A page ev'ry sentence contained,
So an estimate true of your letter
   By figures alone can be gained.

Poor sentences but under-rate it
   And only their feebleness show,
Perchance I can best illustrate it
   By giving an instance or so.

To hear of a victory glorious,
   When victory hangs by a thread,
Makes the coolest of people uproarious—
   Or strikes on their nerves like a dread.

A line from a friend at a distance,
　Whose fortunes in youth were a part
Of your dreams—ay, your very existence—
　Takes a strong, mighty hold on the heart.

The picture of one who has vanished
　To the Beautiful Isles of the Blest,
Whose image we've fancied long banished,
　Wakes memories wild in the breast.

A song like a spell when you heard it,
　Which filled you in youth with delight,
Which swept o'er the spirit and stirred it,
　Still stirs it with mystical might.

The sight of a bush or a bramble,
　Which minds one of childhood and home,
Both with rapture and pain makes us tremble
　When friendless and lonely we roam.

So 'tis not the great things that move you,
　They cannot get into the heart,
But the small things of life come to prove you,
　And never from mem'ry depart.

The smiles or the faint little glances,
　From eyes that we tremble to see,

Are the fountains of all our romances—
　　They charm us wherever we be.

But the sweetest small thing worthy mention,
　　O'erflowing with mem'ries of bliss—
Of influence past comprehension—
　　Is the true mother's every day kiss.

Much of this, I have mentioned, your letter
　　Awoke in a moment in me,
Hence I say it was chuck full of matter
　　And sweets, as the hive of the bee.

Suffice it to say, when I read it,
　　My mem'ry went back through the years
To the time when my first prayer I said it,
　　With innocent trembling and tears.

And I rambled from vista to vista,
　　With remembrance from scene unto scene,
Poked slowly to school with my sister,
　　When I went to old " Dab " at the " Green."

Then I see she goes safe to Miss Tatum,
　　At Shepherd's I'm safe, too—asleep—
Those school days return and I hate 'em,
　　They plowed in my mem'ry so deep.

Alas! for the urchin who hitches
  The beautiful dreams of his youth
To the cruel remembrance of switches,
  Youth's rapture it changes to ruth.

Of course, when the rascal is lazy
  And stubborn—why, whip and be done,
But a despot is he, fierce and crazy,
  Who governs with hickory alone.

To these add the days of McMullen:
  Great heavens! was ever a boy
So truant—so wilful—so sullen—
  So denied ev'ry chalice of joy.

But the gloom of those days had their stories,
  Like lamps through a labyrinth swung
Were the days all bespangled with glories,
  When I sat under Dan'l B. Young.

Their light reaches clean to the present,
  And softens the cares of today,
For the man was so honest and pleasant
  I delighted his beck to obey.

When stern he was likewise consistent,
  When cold he was just to a hair,

Nor familiar, nor haughtily distant,
   Nor of gay nor of cynical air.

Those days were like blossoming fezzans
   In the waste of those other school days,
And appeared like a radiant presence,
   Which nothing but kindness displays.

Old Carlos, that best of best teachers,
   Comes in for a share of good will
And fond recollection, whose features,
   After long years, are beautiful still.

For they brighten as one waxes older,
   Have increasing, not vanishing tints,
For the man was a character moulder,
   Who did what he did like a prince.

His maxim : " With knowledge give pleasure,
   To the head bring the heart as a bride ;"
While the boy seeks Pieria's treasure
   Euterpe should sing at his side.

Thus out through the curious mazes
   Of childhood and boyhood I go,
Through all the queer changes and phases
   Of pivotal rapture and woe.

And those solemn scenes I revisit,
  When loosed from mamma's apron strings,
I thought 'twould be wondrous exquisite
  To fly forth on untrammeled wings.

And those solemner scenes while at college,
  Where pitted 'gainst giants, I strove
In the struggle for honors and knowledge,
  And sometimes for pleasure and love.

And those solemnest scenes of a life time,
  When donning the jacket of gray,
I pined through that terrible strife time
  As fortune and hope fled away.

Thus mem'ry, a mighty magician,
  Aroused by that magic of yours,
Has made me revisit in vision
  Not only Plutonian shores,

But also life's happiest Aidens,
  Where none but good angels remain,
And innocent matrons and maidens
  Penelope's virtue retain.

I thank you, young 'Missus,' for using
  Your wand of enchantment so well,

And I trust, while your patience abusing
  With this whangdoodle twang of my shell,

You'll lock up the doors of hard judgment,
  And cross to the hall o'er the way,
Where Charity sweet has her lodgment,
  And what she suggests you may say.

But judge me in haste or at leisure,
  Severely or gently, dear Suse,
I shall leave it the same to your pleasure,
  Believing you'll give me my dues.

In making my rough retrospection,
  Some mem'ries, untrammeled as yet,
Awaken the fond recollection
  Of faces I cannot forget.

Thus a glance at your writing, reminds me
  Of one just as lovely as you,
And her memory as tenderly binds me
  Today as her charms used to do.

I felt it was almost a duty
  To offer devoirs at her shrine,
Not because of her excellent beauty,
  But because of her spirit divine.

When love was my loveliest passion,
  And eyes like your own made it blaze,
Her wand had a perfect persuasion—
  Her smile was the light of my days.

She dwelt by the noted Catawba,
  And made it more noted to me,
Who dwell by the babbling Cahaba,
  That talks of the dear used-to-be.

And others and others whose letters
  Were charming and honest like yours,
I see them, while forging their fetters,
  Preparing to kick me out doors.

Thus a little hand-writing can prove us,
  And carry us back to the past—
To shrines which we thought could not move us,
  Tho' their spells bound us one time so fast.

Ah, 'tis wonderful after such changes
  The phantom's of youth will arise,
Tho' absence the spirit estranges,
  Their coming finds welcome in sighs.

But, missus, I pray you excuse me,
  I'm down in the ashes at times,

And I hope you'll not blame or abuse me
  For talking about it in rhymes.

And, missus, you ought to consider
  That mem'ry's an unruly shrew,
And waits not to do what we bid her,
  But does what she wishes to do;

Uninvited pops into the noddle,
  With terrible ghosts in her train,
And makes, in a jiffy, a muddle
  Of all the bright thoughts of the brain.

When thus she has scattered our forces,
  She does as she pleases, of course,
And brings in her sprites from all sources,
  And reason surrenders perforce.

She may come with a beautiful bevy
  Of phantoms of days once so bright,
Whose mission seems only to levy
  A tribute on present delight.

She may come with a cluster of faces
  Too charming long since to the boy,
All differing in lines and in graces,
  Yet grieving while glowing with joy.

She may come with a flourish of banners,
　　With squadrons both solemn and gay,
With armies that cover savannahs,
　　With horsemen on scout and foray.

She may come with a mournful procession,
　　Overshadowing victory's train,
One exultant and one in depression,
　　One laughing, one weeping in vain.

Howe'er she may come, I am ready,
　　Her phantoms I still recognize,
And they shake not my spirit, fair lady,
　　But take me, I own, by surprise;

And cause me, in writing, to ramble
　　From subject to subject, like you
At the Fair, in that jumble and scramble,
　　To take in the world at one view.

And I find as much satisfaction,
　　I reckon, while making my round
'Mongst her phantoms, in wrapt retrospection,
　　As you at the Fair ever found.

But I made up my mind not to bore you
　　By giving my serious views,

But to lay out my fardels before you,
    And leave you to pick and to choose.

In doing the one or the other,
    Sweet Charity stands, like a judge,
To warn us confronting our brother,
    Not over right's limits to budge.

She constantly whispers of duty,
    "Good sense," day by day, is her theme;
"True honor 's" her sample of beauty;
    Integrity—this is her dream.

She cries from the housetops to mortals,
    Who struggle and wrangle below:
"Look up toward the love opened portals,
    And kindness and mercy bestow.

"See things in the world as they should be,
    Undarkened by sorrowful mist;
See men at their best, as they would be,
    If they had not so much to resist.

"See glorious deeds in the struggle—
    Not madness alone or despair—
Suspicion eschew, and to juggle,
    Despise it, as mean and unfair.

TO A FRIEND.

We think these days are full of gloom,
   And pray they'll come no more,
But better times will never come
   Than those of Heretofore;
That blessed Heretofore, my boy,
   From first to last was gold,
With just enough of rude alloy
   In one, its parts to hold.

Today we cannot turn our eyes
   Without beholding care,
And even in our clearest skies
   Some specks of sorrow are;
Some specks that seem to grow, my friend:
   And stir they not our fears?
Lest life in darkness yet may end—
   In darkness, doubt and tears.

Let's cherish them, the joys we have,
   Though but a paltry store,

And face our cares with heart so brave
  That we shall conquer more ;
More joys, more hopes, more faith, my boy,
  And see, fresh from the tomb,
The ashes of the days gone by,
  New glories rise and bloom.

EPISTLE TO A FRIEND.

Dear friend, it has been known full well,
That fortune's choice things ne'er yet fell
On spots where I was wont to dwell—
      They seem to dodge me;
But 'gainst my luck I ne'er rebel,
      It doesn't budge me.

I keep straight on from day to day,
At times too sad, at times too gay,
December now, tomorrow May—
      But wav'ring not;
Shifting and veering to obey
      My wonted lot.

'Tis want of money, it may be,
That keeps me skipping like a flea,
But till the bounds of honesty
      I overleap,
My good friends need not frown at me—
      Nor I feel cheap.

Though not sustained—I don't deny it—
By filthy lucre (horrid diet!
For one can't boil, or stew, or fry it;
        Nor, as I fancy,
Can science to a sore apply it—
        Nor necromancy),

Yet I've a lot of jewels rare,
And they are altogether fair,
And so pass muster everywhere—
        In cot or palace;
Content I take these as my share
        From fortune's chalice.

'Tis not the goodly food we eat—
The luscious fruit, the juicy meat—
That makes us manly on the street—
        They help, 'tis true,
To give us nimble hands and feet,
        Our work to do.

'Tis not the kind of mansion, not
The haughty palace or the cot
Most humble, where we spend our lot,
        Which you and me
Is wont to mold and make us what
        We are, should be.

They have their special influence
And modify our life's events ;
They give a color too, perchance,
   To our cheeks and lips ;
But on life's current deep, intense,
   They are but chips.

The unseen—through its vehicle,
The seen—doth things mysterious well,
And by a road we cannot tell
   Doth make us go,
Of thought most fearful is the spell
   For joy or woe.

The mastery of the soul is what
Makes man abhor to be forgot,
And from the standpoint of his lot
   To look up higher
Than flesh : tow'rds some Elysian spot
   Still to aspire.

So what we are or wish to be,
Our neighbors nearest, scarcely see,
Except that some are poor like me,
   Or rich like you ;
Beyond this wealth or poverty
   All is hid from view.

——12

I know beneath my humble roof
There is a shrine, and there, aloof
From base allurements, I make proof
    Of virtuous life :
'Tis well, since 'tis to my behoof
    To escape from strife.

Your pardon, if I thus have writ
Too much : I tried by rhyming it
To give it terseness, if not wit;
    And to win your praise,
And make you write to me a bit
    Some of these days.

WRITTEN TO SAM ROBERTSON, JR.

Be your watchword forever and ever,
  Not upward, but onward, my boy;
Like the tide of the deep, flowing river,
  Bearing burdens along like a toy.

Not upward, still yearning and yearning
  For laurels which, captured or won,
Lie around you as objects of spurning
  To hamper the courses you run.

Not upward, but onward, for honor
  Is not in the stars, but the dust,
With sackcloth and ashes upon her
  Her armor all darkened with rust.

Go snatch her from sackcloth and ashes,
  From nooks where she's wonted to hide,
Kiss the tears from her beautiful lashes,
  And make her your darling and bride.

What do fardels avail, which by nature
    We never were formed to enjoy,
Which harmonize not with our stature,
    And nature's rare moulding destroy ?

Go forth as to struggle and scuffle
    With evils below, not above,
And keep not your head in a muffle,
    And hide not your hand in a glove.

Not upward—for that's a delusion,
    But onward—for there is the light;
Know, the bayonet puts to confusion,
    While shells in the air scarce affright.

With your heart and your head well-directed,
    Your feet in the right way must run,
You'll go downward when Duty's neglected,
    But upward when Duty is done.

FOLLOW YOUR BENT.

One man may be an author rare,
  Another but a scribe who writes
His praises; fitted to declare
  The excellence of his flights—
The author and his critic each,
From diff'rent standpoints, notice reach.

One man may be a sculptor famed,
  Another but his copyist,
By both the same green bays are claimed,
  And both may keep their tryst:
Yet if both win, as win they may,
They do so in a diff'rent way.

One man may be a painter true,
  Another but a dauber vile,
The dull world taken through and through,
  The latter wins awhile;
The world at first must have its way,
Then merit enters in to stay.

Each man seems born for special work,
    Not made to win in ev'ry race;
In the dark world each has his spark
    To light him to his place.
If this, before this place be found,
Goes out, he goes his way uncrowned.

The goal we seek may be the same,
    Tho' far apart the roads we tread ;
The crown, too, has a diff'rent name
    To suit a diff'rent head.
The crown which wakes your ecstacy,
A thorn crown on my brow might be.

Your path was blazed for you, not me,
    My path was blazed for me, not you ;
We'll meet at last beyond the sea
    When duty pulls us through ;
I trust we'll have no bickerings there
About the kind of crowns we wear.

Development can wonders do,
    And of a half fool make a sage ;
The want of it—sad fate to view—
    The maniac's cell and cage,
Where faculties which make our " stars '
Discordant howl behind the bars.

But all development, which serves
    To unmake the man whom God has made;
The system by its working starves
    Until at length 'tis dead
To all its wonted instincts.   What
The consequence?   A blur, a blot.

Uneducated genius blooms
    And withers wild : a monster still,
Upon life's stage he foams and fumes
    Distraught --en deshabille,
And with his most resistless spell
Flings in a dash of hateful hell.

Who keeps his birthright, heritage,
    Endowment, or whate'er it be,
That stamps him as a wight or sage
    Of low or high degree :
Who makes of it the most he can—
That is the most deserving man.

Then go your way, my brother, go
    Where heaven directs your course to be,
With true conviction labor, though,
    In high or low degree;
Then when the roll of honor's read
You'll get a crown to suit your head.

TO STELLA.

ON GIVING HER TENNYSON'S POEMS.

When his human voice no longer
  Is re-echoed through the hall,
And his weird strain wakes us not again
  To joy or sorrow's call,
Then the echoes of his magic,
  Like an inspiration spoke
Thro' the realms of time, will breathe sublime
  To all English-speaking folk.

Hear the great old poet's numbers
  Babbling like a silver stream,
Let their pleasing spell in mem'ry dwell
  Like the witch'ry of a dream.
Then, perchance, at length thy spirit
  May awaken like a bird,
And a song of thine, though less divine,
  Shall be marvelous to be heard.

Thou mayst never sing like Norton,
  Nor like Barrett shake the soul,
But one burning thought to utterance wrought
  May adown the ages roll.
And thy strains may serve to waken,
  It may chance, a lofty aim,
Or to light the fire of purpose higher
  In the struggle after fame.

All who teach our hands a cunning,
  Or our lips to sing anew,
Or sustain the hope with woe to cope,
  Or our paths with pleasure strew—
Breathe like him an inspiration
  Like some earthly Israfel,
And the poet's claim demand of fame,
  Tho' it bring no immortelle.

There is not a field of labor
  But some honor in it lies,
More the arm that wields the sabre
  Than the metal wins the prize.
It may ne'er have seen Damascus,
  By some humble smithy made;
Seems it modestly to ask us
  By a true arm to be swayed.

Ah, the bulwark of our temple
   Is the manhood of her sons,
Whose devoutness, by example,
   Through their daily living runs.
Not because they're known to story
   Not by reason of great deeds;
But because their country's glory
   From their work well done proceeds.

THE SPEECH THAT WE LOOKED FOR THAT NIGHT NEVER CAME.

Read before the Jeffersonian Club—1892.

[James E. Hawkins on the night set for his address before the Jeffersonian Club appeared and apologized for not being ready by claiming that he had studied his subject very thoroughly, had written it out elaborately, and had desired to read it, but that he had taken it with him to the Bar Association at Point Clear, and by some bad luck had left it down there. He delivered, however, an excellent off-hand talk which won applause. Whenever he made a balk he laid it all on the Bar Association and his bad luck in leaving his speech at Point Clear.]

We knew he was able to give us a talk,
   We knew he was witty and smart,
And we never once dreamed that the fellow would
    balk,
   When once we had helped him to start:
By rounds of applause and encouraging smiles,
By all kinds of flattering, popular wiles,
And by coming together to hear him orate
On the scenes of the past in his county and State,
And by linking with other proud worthies his name—
But the speech that we looked for that night never
    came.

Yet when he arose with dignified mien,
  He ne'er was a diffident bore;
I am free to confess that my appetite keen
  Grew sharper than ever before.
For while he was hemming—in face getting red—
I fancied ere long he'd go forging ahead,
And every good hit that he staggered upon
Convinced me the more we were in for the fun,
For he still beat the bushes persistent and game—
Yet the speech that we looked for that night never
    came.

First he swore he had written a speech and all that,
  To suit the occasion when here,
But took it away to the gulf and forgot,
  At the club, he must make his *Point Clear;*
That the thoughts of his head and his paper should
    each
Contain the ingredients of the same speech;
The same rosy fancies, the same witty gleams,
The same shrewd discussions of every day themes;
But not so—he confessed his forgetting with shame—
And the speech that we looked for that night never
    came.

He either forgot to remember, he thought,
  Or remembered, perhaps, to forget:

He couldn't tell which, but he owned he was caught.
  He would give us a benefit yet;
He'd give some reporter a chance after all
To print for the club his delectable scrawl,
And he felt when we read what he wrote up here,
To our full satisfaction, he'd make his *Point Clear*,
And show that the man at the bar was to blame—
Still the speech that we looked for that night never
    came.

The unlimited coinage of silver, he said,
  He favored especially now,
He wanted it *free*—here he lifted his head
  And a smile lit the gloom of his brow—
It would lend to the lawyer, the farmer, the clerk,
Some silvery dreams both at play and at work;
And the ring of the dollars such music would make
That Liberty's altars with rapture would shake,
And 'twould help him his speech from the *bar* to re-
    claim—
But the speech that we looked for that night never
    came.

He thought the sub-treasury bill a mistake,
  So the lending of money on land;
That people their principles often forsake
  When on principal only they stand.

He was talking right here in a beautiful strain,
But his thoughts flew away to the murmuring main,
Where his wonderful article lay all incog,
Locked up in a closet with villainous grog :
And a direful confusion his language o'ercame—
And the speech that we looked for that night never
came.

The people were getting suspicious of us—
He alluded, of course, to the dudes—
And they didn't care much if they did have a fuss :
He dreaded all internal feuds.
He wanted to see ev'ry man get his dues—
Here he choked, for the thought seemed the man to
confuse.
He wanted to see, what all wanted to see,
Our party in power, and so it must be
In the speech he had written he argued the same —
But that speech that we looked for that night never
came.

He trusted the masses, he knew they were right,
Though hither and thither they ran,
They would huddle at last with a vote for the white,
And be true to that vote to the man ;
Too often they voted for sentiment's sake,
But railing about it was all a mistake ;

One-tenth of 'em only have axes to grind—
You must talk to their hearts, then, and not to their
    mind;
These remarks got the speaker a round of acclaim—
But the speech that we looked for that night never
    came.

He couldn't speak longer—his place was the bar;
  The spirits there conjured he downed
In a jiffy—but now all his thoughts were ajar,
  Three dollars would bring 'em around—
His papers he meant, not his thoughts, and he knew
If the club would be patient, he'd come up all true,
He'd show us the hell in protection per se,
And the hell in a trade that is perfectly free.
And protection to silver or gold, just the same :—
But the speech that we looked for that night never
    came.

But we democrats pardon this promise's breach,
  So seldom the man is remiss,
Then he shows us by action far more than by speech
  What a genuine democrat is.
He has worked in the front—been a leader of
    weight—
In the solemn conventions of county and state;
Has wrought for the party with spirit and will,

In office or out been a democrat still—
For such then we pledge him to love him the same :—
Though the speech that we looked for that night
    never came.

TAMMANY.

I have read in my day of some wonderful clubs,
    And of wonderful men that were in 'em,
But this beats 'em all for the wonderful rubs
    Men get when a few are "ag'in 'em."
Let 'em come with their influence, come with their
        fame—
    Let 'em come, what is best, with their dollar;
But humble or haughty it seems just the same—
    They may look for the dickens to follow.

Now what is the matter, and where is the rub?
    When a Democrat faithful displeases;
Perchance 'tis an unwritten law of the club
    That nought but a victim appeases.
Can't some one—won't somebody—take me aside,
    Nor ever be guilty of treason,
And tell me when Democrats true are denied,
    If 'tis founded on fancy or reason?

Let's suppose there are matters for better or worse,
    Ay, wrongs that have never been righted,

——13

Let ev'ry one come and his sorrows rehearse,
  Let none think his thinking is slighted.
Thus we'll settle all matter of weighty import
  In gen'rous exchange of opinion,
And we'll all get together, in some way or sort,
  To fight for the white man's dominion.

As for me, when I look at the prospect ahead,
  How it bristles with arrows to wound us:
When I hearken the stealthy, insidious tread
  Of the foes that are gathering 'round us:
When I think of the schisms and heresies strange,
  Now tearing our party asunder,
Of this tariff-ic grip, and this revenue mange,
  And this vile rage for boodle and plunder:

When I look at the hordes that are homeless and rude,
  That sullenly gather about us,
Just waiting occasion for riot and feud,
  And rejoicing when enemies flout us:
When I look at the slums of the cities around,
  At the furnaces, mines and plantations,
Who bide them in silence just waiting the sound
  Of the trumpet to tell their occasions:

I think it high time we should get ev'ry man
  That is willing to join and abet us,

And fight thus united as well as we can
  'Gainst the evils which darkly beset us.
Your experience and wisdom we need, we should say,
  To the heroes of many a tussel,
And turning to those that are fresh in the fray,
  We need you to pull and to hustle.

So I look from this close, where so few write their
    names,
  To each beat where our banner is planted,
And own I am quick to acknowledge their claims,
  To be ranked with the true and undaunted;
I know they've been true when we needed them sore,
  And still they'll be true when we try 'em,
But fiercer than tigers when turned from our door,
  Henceforth we may never get nigh 'em.

So I stretch forth my hand, with my heart beating
    there,
  To welcome all shoulder to shoulder,
And require of 'em only my fortune to share,
  For glory or shame, like a soldier.
I stretch them my hand with abundant regard,
  And a welcome both honest and hearty,
And say to each comer, "here's at you, old pard,'
  For the honor and toils of the party.

When I conjure the ghosts of the terrible past,
  To give to my people a warning :
To show them the clouds that are gathering fast,
  They listen impatient and scorning.
When I pray them consider the glory—the power—
  That stays with a people united,
And find them unheeding, or bitter, or sour,
  Or worse, to a prejudice plighted ;

I wonder if deafness and blindness of mind
  Appear not at times epidemic,
Transported about on the wings of the wind,
  And smiting the brain, not the "stommic ;"
And I wonder if envy, like fierce Yellow Jack,
  In its season is not pestilential,
And if Satan, in fooling old Eve from the track,
  Didn't mark on the fruit "confidential."

And I wonder if all are not sometimes possessed
  With some sort of demon or devil,
Who gets up among us confusion—unrest—
  And keeps us unwise and uncivil.
And I wonder if Satan e'er finished a job,
  Which wholly delighted and paid him,
In teaching poor mortals each other to rob,
  Without getting some woman to aid him.*

---

*Mrs. Lease, H. B. Stowe, Bloody Mary, etc.

The masses are stubborn and angry besides,
  The leaders are distant and haughty,
The trickster is happy in getting "divides,"
  And the seekers for office are naughty.
But the battle for change of some sort, it is on,
  And the "ins" must now look to the borders,
Their pickets are pressed, will they never lie down?
  But wait like a "greeny" for orders.

Will they never lie down? as they once used to do,
  These fighters, whose names are in story,
When the squads of the gray met the hordes of the
    blue.
  And battled for vict'ry, not glory;
Can't they see what's around, can't they hear what is
    loud,
  How the storm gathers faster and faster?
Will they now play the braggart—be haughty and
    proud,
  And court a defeat—a disaster?

ELEGY.

In a bright and sounding dell
  A clear, wild streamlet rolls,
While far away a sweet, low bell
      Mournful tolls.

Merry yesterday we stood,
  Where the laughing waters beat,
And sang a gay song to the flood
      At our feet.

Now sadly to the echoes swell
  Our sorrow-stricken souls,
To the echoes of the sweet, low bell
      Which tolls.

" Gone, forever gone "—the rill
  Repeats them on its shoals,
And sad the big mouth of the hill
      Half tolls.

Mourners mute march down the wood
  Where flows the laughing wave,
The merry but the mocking flood
  At the grave.

A pall is lain upon the dell,
  An awe the smothered sigh controls,
As the wild wave laughs, and low the bell
  Mournful tolls.

Oh, lay him down and break the spell
  Which thus enchains our minds and souls
As we list, the stream which down the dell
  Laughing rolls.

As we list, the mournful sounding bell
  Keeps saying, " gone," to our sad souls,
When the cruel sod into his cell
  Falls and rolls.

Ah, the cold clay clods that fill the cell,
  They lie as cold upon our souls,
And a wild wail follows when the bell
No longer murmurs thro' the dell,
  Nor tolls.

TO BELLE.

Thy fortune it must change, darling,
   With the shifting waves of life,
Dark rocks of woe will turn life's tide
   And stir the foam of strife.
But ev'ry change thy fortune knows
   Will find the same in mine,
For oh, the waters of my soul
   Are blended, love, with thine.

From joy to joy I've run, darling,
   Chasing the gaudy thing,
And whene'er I caught, it others shared
   Till it had taken wing.
But while I've run from care to care,
   Not chasing—nay, but chased—
I have found me flying all alone
   With unavoiding haste.

While tasting joy and pain, darling,
　Some notions have I caught,
That the only friends in ev'ry fate
　Are those by wisdom brought :
(But alas, too oft the future scene
　It besets with ghostly elves)
Joy may make us love our neighbors best,
　Pain makes us love ourselves.

TO BELLE.

Thou dost not know the sacred flame
　　Which lights my bosom's inner shrine :
Yet burns it there for thee the same—
　　　　My heart is thine.

Thou see'st the sullen brow alone,
　　Not the glad cupid's eyes which shine
Whene'er I see thee—hear thy tone—
　　　　My heart is thine.

Beneath my visage stern and cold
　　Doth lurk a passion sweet as wine,
And love that still must go untold—
　　　　My heart is thine.

From gloom we snatch the brightest brand,
　　And purest fire from saddest shrine,
And tend'rest love from roughest hand—
　　　　My heart is thine.

When spring is wet with od'rous dews,
　When summer's glory 's in decline,
And autumn's tears her cheeks suffuse—
　　My heart is thine.

When winter shakes her hoary hairs,
　Yet in her ingle burn and shine,
Sweet fires like these my bosom bears—
　　My heart is thine.

Through all the changes of its days
　That give the world its shade and shine,
By all life's smooth and rugged ways—
　　My heart is thine.

LULLABY—SLEEP, MY BABY.

Sleep, my baby, fair and sweet!
On a steed both strong and fleet,
Papa flies across the hills—
Swims the rivers—fords the rills:
And we for many a day shall moan,
That from his baby papa's gone.

Many a night, sweet baby mine,
For dear papa we must pine,
Never hope to see him more,
When we hear the cannon's roar,
And weeping we must sit alone,
Oh, baby mine, since papa's gone.

Sleep, sweet baby, many a dawn
We shall know that papa's gone;
You will wake, with laugh and smile,
Mamma's sorrow to beguile,
But still she'll sigh and still she'll weep,
For papa's gone—sweet baby, sleep!

Sleep, sweet baby, I and you—
To dear papa will be true—
For his coming, soon or late,
Morn and eve, we'll watch and wait;
And may the angels papa keep—
Through day, through night, my baby, sleep.

Sleep, my baby, after while,
Just to see his baby smile,
And to take us in his arms,
Papa, tired of war's alarms,
And from the soldier's duties free;
Will come to baby and to me.

Sleep, my baby, many a night,
Though the stars be sweet and bright,
At our door and window pane,
They in cheer shall beam in vain;
While I my loving vigils keep
Above your couch, sweet baby, sleep.

Sleep, sweet baby, many a day,
'Mongst the flowers you shall play;
Or about the cozy hearth,
Through the winter roll in mirth;
While papa pines, in sorrow deep,
For me and you—sleep, baby, sleep.

Sleep, my baby, you'll forget,
Ere the autumn moons have set,
Papa, who is praying now,
With the night dews on his brow,
That vigils o'er us angels keep
By day—by night; sweet baby, sleep.

THE BRAVE AND TENDER.

As being flesh and blood, how can
This earthiest of the earthy—man—
    In his best condition
    Scarce the definition
Of bliss pronounce, or clearly scan?
  Of such his thought and information,
  Must be a kind of inspiration.

How can he estimate the long
And short of knowledge, or the wrong
    And right of pleasure,
    By his little measure;
Or draw the line 'twixt weak and strong?
  The scientist's investigation,
  At best, is but approximation.

So I have deemed that logic best
Which makes in man two things the test:

The brave and tender—
Not mental splendor—
Of happiness the worthiest.
Yet these, too, often are attended
With intelligence, both strong and splendid.

REBIE'S SONG.

Oh, robin, robin, robin,
Sing to a little child,
Oh, robin, robin, robin,
Sing to a little child :
Thus o'er and o'er my Rebie
My lonesome hours beguiled,
And listening half enchanted
To the chorus of the child,
I fancied I could hear and see
Sweet robin red breast on the tree,
Singing of heaven to her and me.

Oh, robin, robin, robin,
Sing to a little child,
Oh, robin, robin, robin,
Sing to a little child.
The autumn leaves are falling,
There's neither grass nor flower
To call the tuneful red breast
——14

From out his silent bower;
  Yet, like an echo, through the air
  Came an answer from the woodland bare—
  A robin red breast carolled there.

    Oh, robin, robin, robin,
      Sing to a little child,
    Oh, robin, robin, robin,
      Sing to a little child:
Thus unpremeditated
  Let me lift up my song,
And call upon the angels
  To sing my path along;
    And answering to my ceaseless guess,
    May they coming make their home and rest
    In my inhospitable breast.

REBIE'S SONG.

TOMORROW WILL COVER TODAY.

When weary I climb to my cot on the hill,
  As the shadows of twilight appear,
And the levers and wheels of the city are still,
  Or their murmurs fall soft on the ear;
What a dreamy emotion, I cannot explain,
  Comes my weariness stealing away,
As my little one sings, in her half weird strain:
  "Tomorrow will cover today."

I listen delighted, but shamed by her song—
  If you'd call it a song that she sings—
And I wonder what fashions the words of her tongue
  Whence the mystical utterance springs.
Perchance they are brought by ethereal birds,
  As a snatch from their own heav'nly lay,
And she keeps on repeating those mystical words:
  "Tomorrow will cover today."

Then I wonder if ever she thought of the thought,
  Thus uttered deep hidden yet clear,
Like fountains of waters from dark caverns brought,
  Both the spirit and body to cheer.
And the wonderment grows, as my little one skips,
  In half dreamy, half frolicsome way,
While ever and ever there springs from her lips:
  "Tomorrow will cover today."

Yes, today, like the leaves of the flowers, will die,
  And the woes of today and its fears
To the land of oblivion haply may fly,
  Nor remain save in memory's tears:
And a bird will keep singing, as prompted by dreams,
  Those birds from the sweet far away,
There's an ocean ahead to receive all the streams;
  "Tomorrow will cover today."

Ah, those ringlets of gold, what a pallet is theirs,
  For glory, for love, and for peace:
And that beautiful face, which no sorrow-trace wears,
  And those cheeks like two bloomy peach trees;
When discord and worry are running one mad,
  Be your magic around me, I pray,
And those lips, with that song, both so weird and glad;
  "Tomorrow will cover today."

May ye all, like the exquisite strains of a song,
    Each lend you enchantment in part;
The tresses and eyes, just as well as the tongue,
    Be as wizards to charm soul and heart,
For I fancy they hint of the glories to be,
    Of the light of a sweet far away;
And they almost persuade me there's part prophecy
    In "Tomorrow will cover today."

Tomorrow is near us, but never an eye,
    Save the prophets, has seen it is as yet;
But when from this scene we have turned with a sigh
    Of mingled delight and regret,
And this sin load, this burden, we've carried so long,
    On the cross of the Savior we lay,
We shall sing, with my little one, her weird song:
    "Tomorrow will cover today."

We shall know then, perchance, what we think we
      now know,
    What the lips of a baby can teach:
How the angels, betimes, on those pure lips bestow
    A beautiful mystical speech.
Why, "Of such is the Kingdom of Heav'n," we'll see,
    When with faith, not with reason, we pray;
And when, like my little one, haply we be--
    "Tomorrow will cover today."

SEWAII.

Hawes drowned his little girl in East Lake.

The night hawk sits beside the lake,
  And screams and trills, and trills and screams,
And all the wild fays of the brake
Sad echo's mystic halls forsake,
And low, mysterious murmurs make,
  The very night wind solemn seems.

The night hawk hides in densest shade,
  And trills and screams, and trills and screams,
The merry noises of the glade,
Of night's rude choristers invade,
His wild-voiced haunt but all are made
  To swell his plaintive woe, it seems.

Now off their silvery finger tips
  The bright stars shake the silv'ry dews,
The sweet flow'rs in their rosy lips
Catch them or ere they find eclipse
In the dark lake, whose billow whips
  The banks whereon I trembling muse.

And this is beautiful and sweet;
    But oh, the night hawk sits and moans,
And sadder seem the murmurous feet
Of dancing billows, as they beat
Against each other and retreat—
    The night hawk hath such weird tones.

It is a lovely night, and things
    Of beauty now themselves should show,
Music should spread her siren wings
And visit Love's Idalian springs,
And Mirth should dance while Orpheus sings,
    And gloom to gloomiest cavern go.

But hark ! the night hawk's voice of woe
    Dispels the sweetness from the air,
And ev'ry scene—above, below—
The winds which " silver sandaled " go,
The waves which dance, the stars which glow,
    Tonight seem smitten of despair.

The night hawk in the brake was stirred,
    A dark form from the wood emerged;
    Pale was his face, his look was weird:
    Had he been list'ning to the bird?
    " Stranger," said I, " you, too, have heard
What ev'ry other sound hath dirged.

"You, too, like me are wan and pale;
    The saddest, wildest notes of woe
That night hawk utters, like a wail
The night hawk—ah! the night hawk's tale
Wakes all the demons of the vale."
    He answered, "Yes, yes, it is so."

"Tonight," said I, "the bodeful bird
    Has in his dying plaint a cry—
A scream, perhaps—and it has stirred
My blood to curdling."   "Tut! absurd!"
The stranger answered, "You are scared!"
    Yet demons hurtled from his eye.

"Well, maybe 'twas a fancy wild,
    The bird seems ever and anon
To whimper like a chill-struck child,
And by his plaint I've been beguiled
Into half frenzy."   Then he smiled,
    "Out on such madness, out, begone!"

Quoth he, "You rave, 'twas but a bird;
    I heard the whimper and the wail,
But had no phantasies absurd.
Ha! ha! I was a moment stirred,
As all are when a plaint is heard
    In such a damp and dismal vale;

"By such a ghostly lake as this,
    In such a lonely, horrid brake.
See how the moon doth trembling kiss
The trembling waters, and I wis
You fancy that you hear a hiss
    From yonder harmless water snake.

"But I—I have no fancies, I
    Delight in screams and hisses—groans
Have never shaken me.   The sigh
Alone disturbs me—'tis the cry
Of speechless, smothered agony,
To which we cannot make reply ;
    An utt'rance from one's very bones."

"The dog's low whine," said I, "the shrill
    Defiance of the mean night hawk,
And of the am'rous whip-poor-will ;
The sad low wooing by the rill
In the deep woods, when all is still,
    To me are almost human talk.

"And on a night like this, the wail
    Or whimper, like that of a child
Half smothered, cause my limbs to quail,
And for a while my heart to fail :
But, man, you look so ghastly pale."
    Quoth he, "Your madness runs me wild."

Then sudden went he as he came,
  He was so death-like pale and wan,
He put the white moonlight to shame,
And gave another pictured name
To death's weird ghostliness, the same
  That horror leaves the face upon.

And on my spirit and my brain
  A wond'rous stupor fell; the bird
Was gone, and yet the mystic pain,
That smote me with each throbbing strain,
I almost yearned to feel again -
  To stupor pain 's to be preferred.

Upon the brain this stupor fell,
  Upon the heart, the pulse, it lay,
And held them like a potent spell:
And which was which I scarce could tell;
Feeling and thought were mixed so well—
  But man and bird had flown away.

The man and bird were gone, alas!
  Their mem'ry it was left behind;
The moonlight dallying with the grass,
Skirting the waters clear as glass,
Seemed sadder than it ever was,
  Before that sad night, to my mind.

The very night winds seemed to come,
  Their mouths wide open, full of woe,
Full freighted from the realm of gloom,
To hint of mystery and doom ;
And I alone sat dark and dumb,
  Nor was ashamed that it was so.

Yet all confused and mystified
  As were my senses there and then,
I felt and with no little pride
My fancy had not wholly lied,
Cause for th' effect suspicion spied,
  Reason assumed her throne again.

Quoth I, " The wailing that I heard,
  It was the wail of one distressed."
Quoth fancy, " It was but a bird."
Suspicion said, " The thing occurred
Before, not after, he appeared."
  Quoth reason, " I will make a quest."

So stealing softly through the brake,
  Of ev'ry noise I was afraid ;
I left the demon haunted lake,
Nor dared a backward glance to take,
Lest on the marge I'd see a snake—
  And, lo! the man was just ahead.

He had been watching me—he fled.
 I saw him, but I heard him not;
As noiseless as a ghost his tread;
'Twas he, not I, now sore afraid—
'Twas he, not I, now sore dismayed—
 I quick pursued—all else forgot.

I saw him, now I saw him not;
 He passed the old deserted mill;
Across the bridge he leaped, he shot—
And I pursued him fast and hot,
But lost him in the willow grot.
 I turned me breathless down the rill.

 * * * * * * * *

Five senses, ministers, have we—
 Sight, hearing, feeling, taste and smell:
There may perchance another be,
Which localizes mystery
With vision kin to prophecy,
 Keen to detect th' enchanter's spell.

It may be in the depths of lore,
 Hid in its labyrinths; we may yet
Detect it and its laws explore,
As combination, if no more,

Of all, perchance, and full of power,
    Woven together like a net.

This vision read for me the face
    Of what had been a man, now fiend ;
And clue by clue, and trace by trace,
Went after him from place to place :
Beheld this Catalinean pace—
    And from all, accusation gleaned.

Out on the city's highland rim,
    And in the alley's dang'rous haunts,
The cheering lamps were growing dim,
As o'er a bright eye falls a film ;
The dark'ning shadows seemed to swim,
    And I went through them half in trance.

The man was there, the night hawk there—
    The ghost of what had been a man ;
And ev'ry sound that smote the air
Upon its pinions seemed to bear
Part of the night hawk's voice of care,
    And chilling through the veins it ran.

And ever and anon I heard
    The whine and whimper of a child,
And tried to think my thoughts absurd.

The man had said so: for a bird
Is but a bird, and to be stirred
  By such is folly, almost wild.

The night winds puffing 'gainst my door,
  Or through the lattice sighing wild,
Seemed coming from ghost-haunted shore,
Or from witch-peopled heretofore—
Where souls, in vain bygones deplore,
  Sobbed like the sobbing of a child.

And ev'ry shadow took the form—
  The aspect of the wan, weird man,
And stood before me boding harm,
And like a frail thing in a storm
I cowered before it in alarm,
  And horror through my vitals ran.

There is no Stygian gloom or fret
  Like that of awe benighted souls;
Strange and unwelcome fancies flit
About the spirit, darkening it,
Or on it terrifying sit,
  Like hawks on dove cotes, dark as ghouls.

That night upon my pillow fell
  The shadow of a bird, and sleep

Fled frightened from it, and a spell
Of awe and mystery dark, as well,
Possessed my thoughts—ah, what a hell
    Is fancy loosed from reason's keep.

All sounds transmitted into wails,
    And thousands crowded on the air
Of woe were aggravated tales,
And smote my spirit as keen flails
The naked body smites.   What ails
    The bird with such a voice of care?

What ails the man—the haggard man?
    Who sudden came and sudden went;
Who spoke so brave, yet looked so wan:
What wild emotions wake and ran
Through each heart fibre fitful?   Can
    Remorse be kept forever pent?

*   *   *   *   *   *   *   *

Two nights thereafter, miles away
    From where those strange happened, lone
I sat in darkness—wishing day
Would come with spirit-charming ray;
For mem'ry on me seemed to prey,
    And fancy had a-fevered grown.

A man approached, but saw me not
   In hiding.   So complaint he made :
Quoth he, " A most unhappy lot
Is mine—scenes cannot be forgot—
May fire consume the cursed cot
   Where first my true love was betrayed.

" My child, my child !   The bird, the bird !
   The man !   The lake !   What can I do ?
Where'er I go that wail is heard ;
And then that man with look so weird
And so suspecting : how he leered
   At me, as if my crime he knew."

He vanished muttering—cursing low—
   It was the self same man I met
At Como Lake—who stirred me so.
Said I, " Back thither will I go,
And what has happened there I'll know,
   And eyes upon his pathway set."

*   *   *   *   *   *   *   *

Three days thereafter, up the street
   An ugly crowd, enraged, advanced ;
That man was in their midst.   Full neat
His dress—his nonchalance complete—

He heeded not their anger heat,
  But at them, half in scorn, he glanced.

*   *   *   *   *   *   *   *

Next time I saw him, lone he stood
  To make for life a last defense,
The halter on his neck.   What could
He say?   He caught my eye: the blood
Rose to his cheeks: he pulled the hood—
  The scaffold fell: and he went hence.

THE STRENGTH OF UNITY.

All facts and fancies have significance:
  The greatest are but of the least the sum,
And Nature's lips still argue against chance,
  And use Earth's dull material things and dumb,
To point th' immortal, immaterial Home:
  No thing created wanting influence or
The gift of some expression. The insect's hum,
  And the endless harmony of the glitt'ring star,
  All hint, suggest, declare, a wondrous Creator.

We show our kinship to the First and Last—
  The faultless Architect, the only good,
The only beautiful and unsurpassed—
  By work : by sacrifice of sweat and blood ;
For sweat and blood are one when understood.
  We prove our worthiness by duties done—
In doing brave and God-like what we should,
  By using thread already for us spun,
  By finishing the labor for our hands begun.

We prove our like to the Great First Cause
    By seeing, recognizing, in all things
A cause, which, under fixed, appropriate laws,
    Shows some appropriate, fixed effect, and brings
From Chaos Land what has immortal wings,
    And sends them Canaanward to talk of God..
To all the nations in their wanderings
    We prove ourselves by honoring the sod
    On which Immanuel's blest and wounded feet have
        trod.

Good deeds are always beautiful, and mark
    Our pathway with a patch of roses sweet
As heaven's, tow'rds which our fond hopes, like the
        lark
    Rejoicing in the morn, fly far and fleet.
Good deeds are cheering lamps to wand'ring feet
    And through the fearful darkness, gloom, or mist
Of sin-confusion shine, and it half cheat
    Of its strong terrors—stronger than we wist—
    They alter all our circumstances as they list.

Not one good work of ours is lost in sand;
    And that which chisels things of beauty works
In harmony with God's own faultless hand.
    Thousands since Noah have been building arks

For others than themselves; have built strong barks
  To ride the stormy billows of Life's sea:
Thousands have spent their lives in striking sparks
  To kindle fires for others—you and me.
  A God-like wish was theirs—theirs a like memory.

So what of good we earnest do today,
  Constructs a kind of Cheops' pyramid
For us and ours, when we have passed away ;
  Albeit hieroglyphic, dim and hid
The marvelous meanings be, while buried 'mid
  The weeds and trash of life's environments,
Yet they of such in season will be rid;
  This is the fabled Phœnix of events,
  And hist'ry gets from such her mystic lore and
    tints.

The hands united here, the shoulders bent,
  In common 'gainst a mighty, common foe—
The cheering words to one another lent:
  The merit wit, the loving humor-blow,
The calm, wise words which wisdom's pathway show;
  The social trustfulness and helpful cheer—
The magic of enthusiasm's glow :
  These are the forces that unite us here,
  And manhood's vessel through the rudest breakers
    steer.

Truth from the mouth of simple ones is strong,
  As when proclaimed by judge or senator,
And "Annie Laurie," but a poor love song,
  Becomes to exiled Scots a song of war,
And stirs the dream of burn and brae afar,
  As much as tramping hosts or roaring gun.
A mem'ry or a song may make or mar
  Our joy or peace : may make wide peoples one :
  And simple things developed we must seek or
    shun.

'Tis not the great thing, then, the wondrous work
  We do, that wins and keeps immortal name :
'Tis that which in itself contains the spark
  Of truth, which merits and demands acclaim
From an unwilling, scoffing world, whose blame
  Betimes more eloquent is than its best praise.
This spark of truth is mightier than a flame
  Of fallacy, with all its luring rays,
  Which move not deep, nor melt with genuine magic
    blaze.

The spirit of good counsels prophesies
  The measure of their influence, if the glow
Or beauty of Immanuel glorifies
  And hallows it; and angels only know
The blessings which our labors must bestow.

But if self-seeking, proud ambition move
And guide us, time and circumstance quick show
  Our influence, measured by a narrow groove,
  And that our greatest pow'rs most suicidal prove.

The dark perpetual nimbus of regret
  Broods weeping o'er the path of those who woo
And foster discord. Furies' harpies whet
  Their beaks, and make demoniac ado
About contention's victims, and pursue
  Them by their noise or noisesome rottenness.
To discord all things wear a lurid hue,
  And hope, the last sweet martyr, faints and dies
  When discord breaks the shell whence swell life's
      harmonies.

Keep sentries out to watch this deadly foe—
  This child twin-born with peace ; despised, exiled,
By all good spirits : wand'ring to and fro,
  He seeketh whom he may devour : beguiled
He cannot be nor ever reconciled.
Each winning manner he assumes betimes :
He crawls into our bosom like a child,
He comes in argument—in rosy rhymes—
And out of love's sweet darts makes daggers for his
     crimes.

The strongest forts he must encounter still
   Are cautious moderation, charity.
He hates the portals of a patient will,
His sting distils the honey of the bee,
Instead of poison drops where two or three
Are met in peace.   So let us meet and stand—
   Contribute each some little harmony,
Which, wisely linked, may make a chorus grand
To be the poem or the praise song of the land.

THE DAY.

Day never leaves us altogether
  To inhospitable night,
Where gloom and danger reign, but rather,
  When she's ready.for her flight,
She sprinkles with her stars so bright
  All the threshold of the sky,
To twinkle when she's gone, and night,
  With her ghost-train, to defy.

Day never leaves us altogether,
  But keeps on coming back,
In her due season hither, thither,
  On her glory-haunted track,
To gather up the glittering gems
  Which she left with gloomy even,
As torches, or as diadems,
  When she walked the courts of heaven.

All that is lovely in the night
  Is what she gets from day,
Whose footprints, when she takes her flight,
  Sparkle in the milky way.
The planets are but silver posts
  On the borders of the night,
'Round which the lesser starry hosts
  Keep up their radiant flight.

The full moon blushing floats thro' heaven
  On her star-bespangled way,
Wearing the silver mantle given
  Her by the god of day.
Birds, dreaming in their leafy cotes
  Of some myst'ry of the day,
Half wakeful pipe sweet broken notes
  Of their daytime's passion lay.

MY DEAD.

Oh, that voice so rich and cheery,
   I recall its music yet,
When I went forth wan and weary
   Through the troubles that beset.
How my courage woke and started
   When your accents round me gushed,
Oh, the music that departed
   When in death that voice was hushed.

Touch me now, who may, with fingers
   Sweet as "rosy fingered morn;"
While his spell in mem'ry lingers
   Let their charm to them return.
Sing like siren—ah, wild voices—
   Smile like angels—ah, blest eyes—
But my soul his chiefly prizes,
   And for his forever sighs.

Oh, those big white hands, my darling,
  Which you used to put in mine,
When you found me sour and snarling,
  Or disposed to fret and pine;
How they made me cheerful hearted,
  How they raised my hope and faith,
Oh, the magic that departed
  When they folded cold in death.

Oh, those big blue eyes, my Murray,
  That were ever full of love
When I frowned or sighed in worry,
  O'er thorns beneath and clouds above.
Through my gloom their magic darted,
  Smote me like a heav'nly breath:
Oh, the enchantment that departed
  When their smiles went out in death.

FREEDOM.

SCENE IN COAHOMA COUNTY, MISSISSIPPI, JULY 4, 1865.

Two hundred faces—lacking eight—
  Kind faces all with look subdued,
Like those on which the hand of fate
    Which has not been or harsh or rude,
      Has rested through long, weary years,
      And left on them the touch of tears.

Two hundred faces—lacking eight—
  Looked anxious tow'rds their master's face;
Their thrall had taught them well to wait,
    And in his frown or smile to trace
      Good luck or bad; and yet today
      Their restlessness they could not stay.

A glorious barbecue was spread,
  A rich farm's richest fruit and spoil,
In glad profusion here was laid,
    A partial earnest of their toil:

Yet more than hunger now, it seemed,
Within their kindly soft eyes gleamed.

Perchance there lay a shadow there,
    Perchance expectancy so deep,
It wore the urgency of care,
    And could but from the lashes leap:
        An unseen something talking sweet,
        Which made their pulses restless beat.

But as those ebon faces gazed
    At us with look unwonted, I,
Whose eyes with inner tumult blazed,
    To him my friend drew slowly nigh,
        And at his elbow took my stand,
        And on my pistol lay my hand.

My friend was tall and handsome; fair,
    And touched with roses, were his cheeks;
He had a merry, gallant air
    Such as of conscious courage speaks;
        And if he felt one thrill of fear
        It did not in his face appear.

He had the haughty master's mien,
    Yet pleasant smiles were in his eyes,
Like those which we have often seen

When masters doffed their wonted guise
  Of stern authority, and showed
  The sympathy which 'neath it glowed.

'Twas sure he looked not through my eyes,
  Nor hinted I of what I saw
Or dreamed I saw; through fear's surmise,
  Perchance through momentary awe,
    I fancied angry tones I heard :
    Yet he was cheery as a bird.

And tossing back his golden hair,
  " Attention ! " cried, and so began :
" Before you now my head I bare ;
  Your master for the last time scan.
    No longer you belong to me—
    The war is over, you are free.

" There's not a slave now in this land—
  No master and no negro slaves.
You need not budge at my command,
  Nor mercy at my hand now crave ;
    Your time and labor all are yours,
    Wide open are your prison doors.

" Just nine and eighty years today
  My fathers in convention met,

And one of them was pleased to say
　His heart on Independence set,
　　All men are equal born and free;
　　The others cried, 'So mote it be.'

"I never yet have thought this true—
　I fought to say it was not so.
The white man never was like you;
　Into his sphere you cannot grow.
　　A white man you can never be,
　　Tho' you to doomsday should be free.

"But be this as it may be, free
　You are henceforth; I come to bear
The tidings glad to you; to be
　The first the good news to declare;
　　And as you have been true and tried,
　　To bid you in your homes abide."

We oft and oft the "rebel" yell
　Had heard; the crash and hellish whir
Of solid shot and bursting shell:
　Of furious grape and cannister
　　In woodlands where the battle raged,
　　When nations fight with nations waged:

But never heard we wilder screams
　Than those which rent those cloudless skies,

Nor ever saw we fiercer gleams
  Than those which lit those frenzied eyes :
    Two hundred demons—lacking eight—
    Burst yelling from their prison gate.

They fell into each other's arms,
  A writhing mass of madness : men
Tore garments from each other's forms,
  And wept, and danced, and wept again :
    And men kissed men, while by the throat
    Seizing the women, them they smote.

Mothers in ecstacy of delight
  Tossed up their babes into the air,
Old men and women, wondering quite,
  Looked perfect pictures of despair.
    Young "bucks," their heads together thumped,
    And wild into the bayou jumped.

They snatched the hot meat from the spit,
  And with it smote each other's cheeks ;
Emptied the bread into the pit,
  And in their diabolic freaks
    Kicked o'er the "spread" with rude guffaw,
    And blasphemed everything they saw.

But no, they cursed not him or me,
  Who motionless as pillars stood :

I, nervous and alert; but he,
  In calm but melancholy mood—
    Upon his brow a look of care,
    And in his eyes a dangerous glare.

They cursed not us, two lone white men
  In that dark wilderness complete.
Their madness ended—once again
  They gather slowly at his feet,
    And once again, all mild and meek,
    Most kindly words they haste to speak.

Musing I sat, nor scarcely heard
  The interchange of pleasing talk ;
My soul was deeply, wildly stirred,
  And naught could meditation balk.
    Thus in the dark piazza's shade
    My musings into song I made :

"Oh, liberty ! oh, sweet wild dream !
  How mightier ev'n than Circe's spell
Art thou ; religion's fair twin theme
  On which life's thoughts the longest dwell,
    We suffer ev'ry ill for thee,
    Facing each danger to be free.

" With infancy's first budding thought
  Our nature battles 'gainst restraint:
——16

The last thing to young manhood taught
　('Gainst which he makes the most complaint,)
　　Submission to another's will,
　　·Wakes in proud hearts rebellion still.

" Though training twine her silken chains,
　Little by little, round fierce wills,
And thus each thought and sense constrains,
　And meek obedience last instils :
　　They still resist the tyrant's nod,
　　And own no god to fear but God.

" What captive ever learned to love
　His thraldom ? in its hug so rude
Ambition lies, and seems to prove
　Submissive, if not quite subdued ;
　　Yet studying treason all the while,
　　Looks strategy in ev'ry smile.

" Spirit of freedom ! strange indeed
　The sweet enchantment of thy name ;
Thou, only thou, dost never need
　Muses thy glories to proclaim.
　　To worship thee men are not taught,
　　For they begin it with first thought.

" The swallow swift on flashing wing
　Recalls thy spirit, and the winds,

At each obstruction murmuring,
  In whom the cloud a transport finds,
    Recall thee, and thee typify,
    Far wanderer of earth and sky.

"The imaginations of great souls,
  The unpent flash of genius' flame,
The dream of love which nought controls,
  Nor lash of sneers nor dread of shame:
    These are thy cousins-german—these
    Would thy divinity appease.

"Oh, liberty! man were as nought
  Without thee; thou hast ever been
With him a most abiding thought
  Of self respect, itself the twin.
    Thy spirit animates his veins,
    And snaps like Samson all his chains.

"As 'twere, thou'rt sentry at the gates
  Of all his worthy citadels,
And only when his cruel fates
  Excite thee, despotism dwells
    Secure within them, and the folk,
    Like dastard, wear a servile yoke.

"With thee to guard my cabin door,
  To sit beside my cabin hearth,

I may be ne'er so humble poor,
  But never shall forget my mirth,
    My sense of joy, or hope, or song:
    Life's war I shall with cheer prolong.

"To tread the wine press cheered by thee
  Were not a fate too hard to bear,
And ev'n in banishment to be
  Were not a woe if thou wert there.
    For still there is a hardy joy
    In wastes where chains do not annoy.

"How sweet the airs of dewy morn,
  Fresh from the chambers of the hills,
Wherein the sweet-lipped flowering thorn
  Its most delicious sweets distils;
    And, oh, the chiefest charm to me
    Comes with the sense that they come free!

"How sweet to walk the sounding shore,
  And see the billows heave and dance,
And list the unsyllabic roar
  From out the wide, wide sea's expanse:
    As white caps leap and reel in glee,
    For these at ebb or flow are free.

"Oh, liberty! till Adam fell
  There were no shackles on thy feet,

The notes of ev'ry music shell,
  Thy beauty and thy graces sweet
    Rehearsed in happy paradise:
    Like Eve thou hadst nor sin, nor guile.

" Now we must hedge thee round with arms,
  And pour our precious blood for thee ;
As guard the gallant brave the charms
  Of Eve's fair daughters, so do we
    Encompass with unbroken line
    Of guards thy altar and thy shrine."

So, while I mused upon the throng
  From bonds let loose, from shackles free,
I the occasion did not wrong
  By sneering at their ecstacy
    And their mad antics, but with sighs
    Betrayed my wonted sympathies.

For great emotions, full and strong,
  Had risen up and shut the doors
Of ev'ry utt'rance of the tongue,
  But let loose sighings by the scores—
    While language was a prisoner quite—
    Lest the weak heart should break outright.

A captive have I been of war,
  For months in dismal cells immured,

Where but one sunbeam, like a star,
  The mad'ning darkness pierced and lured,
    The thought benighted and oppressed,
    Up towards its mansion of the blest.

And I have pined in barracks chill
  Begirt by bitter northern snows,
With freedom scarce enough to fill
  My lungs with heaven's free air; so close
    The faithful war dogs watched my ways
    Through horrid nights and dreary days.

I, too, have dreamed, by night, I wore
  Upon my feet—my wounded feet—
The clanking chain : into the core,
  Methought corrosive, it did eat :
    Waking I found 'twas but the thirst
    And hunger which all captives cursed.

So dread were prison bounds by day—
  So on my brain, my nerve, it wrought,
That when the will had lost its sway,
  Fancy with antics strange was fraught,
    And intimated thus the pains
    Man feels by ev'n the dream of chains.

I've seen the prisoner's ev'ry woe—
  The plaintive, fierce; the stern and meek

Seen Samsons sinking, pining slow,
　Day after day, week after week :
　　Seen the heart's canker doff disguise,
　　And sit upon the lip and eyes.

I've set me down, through long, lone nights,
　Beside the bunk, where dying, lay
One who had faced a hundred fights
　And still was ready for the fray,
　　If free to pass the prison door
　　And stride his gallant steed once more.

For freedom pining, sick to see
　The rugged, ragged boys in camp,
To share their fate, whate'er it be—
　The hunger, danger, weary tramp :
　　To obey with them the bugle call,
　　Or in the line with them to fall.

More brave men die of galling chains,
　Of narrow limits, strong confines,
Than do of bodily aches and pains
　At which when free one scarce repines.
　　Care has a royal feast on such
　　As cannot 'scape the prison's clutch.

Alas for him, from cradle days
　A child in woodland nurtured ; reared

Beside the mountain wave, where plays
　　The fox and rabbit, and unscared
　　　The bobolink and robin sing
　　　To greet the sweet buds of the spring.

Where turtles, mockers, thrushes make
　　Love matches, and the mild-eyed cow
Elixir draughts delights to take;
　　And where his horse, free from the plow,
　　　Quenches his thirst with grateful sigh,
　　　In sunshine rolls his master nigh.

That rustic used from balmy dawn
　　To labor till sweet twilight; full
Of vigor, health and active brawn;
　　At noon to lie where waters lull,
　　　In broad beech shade; unfettered still,
　　　Free as the bird, the breeze and rill.

Alas! for him, in army life,
　　So changed from that he knew at home;
From mother torn—it may be wife—
　　No longer free to go or come.
　　　Worse still, if pent in prison cell:
　　　This is, indeed, to him a hell.

How sad his fate, who leaves at morn
　　Bright little faces at the door,

And two dear eyes which look forlorn,
  Lest they may see him nevermore:
    In pride she urges him to fly,
    Yet sees him go with many a sigh.

That peaceful, sunny home of yore
  With dumb lips, as 'twere, says " depart,"
No longer wears the look it wore, ·
  And yet 'tis dearer to his heart :
    A war cloud, danger pregnant, lowers
    Above its one time happy bowers.

And other homes, and other eyes,
  And other interests call him forth,
• They break indeed some olden ties,
  But others weave of greater worth :
    They needed erst his smile's sweet charm,
    But now they need his mighty arm.

But yesterday his words were sweet—
  Today they cry for gallant deeds ;
Then they were charmed by graceful feet
  Or lips that piped on tuneful reeds ;
    Today they ask a lip compressed—
    A steady foot—a dauntless breast.

Thus moved, he cannot, must not heed
  The soft, wild pleadings of love's eyes,

But hearkening to the general need
  'Tis his above base self to rise;
    On maudlin sentiment to frown,
    And tread the earthy sensuous down.

He clasps the dear ones to his breast;
  To her talks hope, and even speaks
Of winning laurels; yet unguessed
  Kisses her brow, her lips, her cheeks,
    And, wiping hot tears from his eyes,
    Leaps on his steed and campward flies.

Ere measuring a score of miles,
  He hears perchance the 'larum gun—
Steals wary on through dark defiles,
  Spurs down the valley in a run,
    He knows his bugle's shrill alarms,
    He knows the long roll's call to arms;

Knows, as it has familiar grown,
  The pickets still increasing fire,
Catches that deep mysterious moan,
  Which floats upon the air, as nigher
    And nigher comes the battle tide;
    Contends with fear, yet follows pride:

Joins in the charge; rides 'gainst the foe;
  With merry madness presses on,

Strikes fast with many a sabre blow
  The squad which will not fly their gun.
    His steed is smitten, falls and dies—
    And he, a gallant captive, lies.

The foe may generous prove and kind—
  The gallantest are ever so—
Yet nought can banish from his mind
  The prisoner's ever present woe :
    That sense of something boding ill,
    Pregnant with terrors, haunts him still.

And worse than this—if aught be worse—
  The thought that friends who saw him fall,
The saddest tidings will rehearse
  To her, and thus her soul appall ;
    And dash the sweet cup of her youth
    With the gall of the bitterest ruth.

He sees the castle of her bliss
  A wreck : he sees those bright sweet eyes
Lose ev'ry glance of joyousness ;
  Those red lips parched with frequent sighs :
    He hears, instead of voices glad,
    Those plaintful—as 'twere, sorrow clad.

The ruddy glories of her face
  He finds by constant drain of tears

To sickly pallor giving place,
As stout hope is dethroned by fears.
Alas ! such fevered thoughts as these
To one in chains are agonies.

But to be all subdued to chains,
To wear the captive's gyves content,
Is worse than all the captive's pains,
Raging in bonds, that may be sent :
The one may but the body kill,
The other overthrows the will.

Vile slavery ! thou art a woe,
A deadly nightmare of the blood,
Eclipsing quite its fiery glow
When once instilled into its flood :
Thou mak'st the sentries of the mind
And soul, to independence blind.

From servile father unto son
Thou dost descend : a soul disease
Through generations thou dost run ;
As fountain waters seek the seas
Where they are swallowed, thus by thee
The soul's best instincts swallowed be.

Thus freedom to the Southern slave,
Though different, in degree,

From that for which all things we'd brave
  And brook on land and sea,
    Is dear and sweet, and in his breast
    Has ever been a dream repressed—
    An object, though, of ceaseless quest.

Trained as he has been to his chain,
  It has hurt him, ne'ertheless :
Upon his pulse of hope has lain
  His aspirings to repress.
    It has dulled his sense of right and wrong,
    And his sense of evil made more strong.

'Tis well that chain is snapped : 'tis best
  Should he, by slow degree,
Develop, under guidance blest,
  A fitness to be free—
    A moral, mental aptitude
    To assimilate this rich, new food.

For freedom is a food, which all
  At first cannot digest ;
There seems a time of proper thrall,
  As for children at the breast
Of mother nature milking—where
    Their stomachs learn strong food to bear,
    And thus for heavy loads prepare.

But freedom, in its mystic sense,
  In mortals is innate—
Inherent—not a thing of chance,
  But a part of their estate.
    Some ne'er enjoy it, but the while
    Some take it to a surfeit vile.

For generations it may sleep:
  It never dies, but bides
Its time—like grasses, buried deep,
  Waiting the suns and tides
    To loose them, and to wake their smile:
    So sleeps it—wakes it—in its while.

The Southern negro's time and tide,
  No doubt, were coming on;
The opportunity denied
  Kept back his freedom's dawn,
    When given by the white man's war,
    The gates for him were set ajar.

    *   *   *   *   *   *   *   *

The twilight shadows came, and found
  Me musing. With them came
A stillness and an awe around—
  A sense without a name—
    But when the broad-winged darkness fell
    Again, the din began to swell.

All night the twang of banjo's string
    And the fiddle's screech was heard,
And back of this, low murmuring,
    Which my spirit wildly stirred;
        But the master of that wide domain
        Was calm, nor showed one touch of pain.

Freedom to natural license ran—
    The negro now was drunk.
Thus his first glory day began,
    And thus, in riot, sunk
        The first hours of his freedom's birth—
        Now he's a nation of the earth.

   *   *   *   *   *   *   *   *

The negro's day has passed away,
    His woes have just begun,
And the mammies of another day
    Their latest web have spun—
        Those mammies, whom as friends we knew
        In all our woes, forever true.

The good old uncles of the past,
    So cordial and polite,
Their merriment was ne'er o'ercast,
    Kind words were their delight.
        A gloom is brooding o'er them now,
        And scowls, not smiles, now wreathe their brow.

No more their songs at eventide
  Burst in the dewy air,
With the echoes of the war it died
  In silence and despair ;
    And where the broken shackle lies
    Heaped o'er it are friendship's broken ties.

Those dear old people of the South,
  Their hist'ry stands alone,
And waits the minstrel's shell and mouth,
  Their glories dead and strewn,
    To sing as poets sing the bowers
    The blast has reft of all their flowers.

So much of tenderness is lost,
  So much of music's best,
So much of all we need the most,
  Felt, known, but unexpressed—
    Like leaves snatched from the parent stem.—
    Is gone—is scattered far with them.

And thro' our hills and valleys mirth
  And song a-moaning go ;
But mem'ry keeps them at her hearth,
  And all their fires aglow.
    And some fond Southron yet will tell
    Their glories on his faithful shell.

THE OLD CONFED.

The old Confed! the Dixie boy,
May all his ways be ways of joy,
And all his paths be paths of peace,
Until his days of troubling cease.

The old Confed! who saw him erst,
When the dark war cloud o'er him burst,
Begirt on every side by fire,
But saw a hero to admire?
Who saw him unbefriended, and
With all the world against him, stand
And look disaster in the face
With calm, chivalric, christian grace;
And did not feel a pleasing awe
Possess his soul at what he saw?
And, on it musing o'er and o'er,
Trust—love--his fellow man the more?

The old Confed of Dixie land!
His courage who may understand?
——17

Who may pronounce his fortitude,
His dauntless heart, his cheerful mood?
In dark encounters with dark foes,
Who ever dealt the sturdiest blows,
And were as brave a band of men
As e'er were whipped and came again?
To whose quick glory be it said,
They fought like men, like heroes bled?
Who saw him wrestling with such odds,
But owned his kinship to the gods?

The old Confed! in trials sore,
Did ever mortal suffer more!
And yet was ever mortal known,
To bear such fate without a groan?
In such privation tempted, tried,
His ev'ry need, not want, denied;
And as the pulse the weaker grew,
The soul a holier impulse knew;
And while his hope seemed to decay,
His faith waxed sweeter day by day;
And while you crushed him to the dust,
In God he put a firmer trust.

The old Confed! 'tis commonplace
To call him bravest of his race;

But what he has been—is—today—
It beggars language to portray ;
For was he not the poorest man,
In ev'rything but pride, clan,
That e'er surrendered sword and gun,
Yet kept his tryst with ev'ry one?
Behold him, when by hunger pressed,
Whom did he plunder in his quest
For food?   And, naked, who asserts
He robbed him of his shoes and shirts?
And homeless, shelterless, and cold,
Who saw him break his neighbor's " hold ?"

The old Confed! with arms in hand,
Trudged like a christian thro' the land,
And cheered the folk his path along,
Seeking his home with mirth and song,
Content to laugh at his own woes :
For mirth his weakness to expose,
To call up scenes of danger fierce
And his partaking to rehearse,
Not with one word of boast or brag,
Nor with the effront'ry of the wag,
But tossing forth his glory crown,
Just as he threw his knapsack down.
So free of care—so full of woe,

Yet all his heart with hope aglow,
He cast no cloud—he left no frown—
But smiling wore his thorny crown.

The old Confed! When all was lost,
Which such dread sacrifice had cost:
Who, coming back, alas! like him,
And finding home lights gone or dim,
Did not in anguish curse and rave,
At those whose hearth he bled to save?
A hero still, he did not so,
But dashed away his cup of woe,
And with no vain repinings, whined
O'er cruel foes or fates unkind,
But like a christian silent shed
His tear—God bless the old Confed!
To his dead brothers' mem'ries true
He built his altars up anew;
True to his Appomattox vow
He turned his sword into a plow,
And went afield, the furrow trod,
And talked with nature and with God.

The old Confed! What did he do?
Those hands, that never hardship knew,
Took up the axe, the plow, the spade,

And homes of peace and plenty made.
Ay, since that day what has he done?
Behold the fabric he has spun,
And then pronounce me, if you can,
If he is not a marvelous man?
In desolation—in the stress
Of mind and body, who may guess
His troublings? He has shown the world
That since his flag in dust was furled,
He still is true, a better man,
Than when tow'rds bristling guns he ran—
Than when its floating in the wind
Spoke of the homes he left behind.

The old Confed! has fought his last,
And reconstruction days are past,
And only now and then he sees
Some wagon train man, ill at ease,
And trembling still, lest he be hurt,
Heroic wave the bloody shirt
(Hearing, perchance, some caterwaul
He fancies it a kuklux call,
And in each vile imposter's tale
Of woe, he hears his country's wail).
Yes, only ever and anon,
Some pension-seeker fires his gun,

But else peace, like the blue above,
Enfolds and kisses us in love.
How fares the old Confederate now?
Beneath his burden does he bow?
(And many an old Confed is worn
And many an old Confed's forlorn)—
Yet tell me, bowed by age and care,
Who hears him whining in despair?

The old Confed! Ah, woe is me,
If I, one fallen, broken, see—
After a moral heroism shown
In peace and war so seldom known—
And pause not pitying, and with hand
With plenty filled, I do not stand,
And so divide—ah, woe is me!
That such neglected e'er should be.
We, on whose paths the roses grow,
If we desert him in his woe,
Shall find each rose conceals a thorn
On which we'll stumble and be torn.
Let's ask ourselves: who comforts him
Now that his life-fire waxes dim?
Must he now cry and cry in vain,
And not a comrade soothe his pain?
Alas! he will not even sigh,

But mute and uncomplaining die.
The same strong spirit, stern and proud,
Burns from the ashes of his shroud :
The same strong spirit, which of yore
Urged him unlaureled on through gore.

The old Confed! may God forfend
That he should ever need a friend ;
He stood beside us in the past,
We'll stand beside him to the last.
So with united voice let's say,
And with united heart let's pray :
" Dear old Confed—dear Dixie boy—
May all thy ways be ways of joy ;
And all thy paths be paths of peace,
Until thy days of troubling cease."

TO MY WIFE.

How could I love thee more than now?
  'Twere virtue turned to sin
If my poor self should fondlier bow
Before thy feet; worse to allow
    More fires to hem it in,
        And stronger chains to twine about
        The guards of Reason's last redoubt.

Why murmur if I do not wear
  A visage glowing sweet
With tell-tale tenderness? 'Tis rare
Majestic love and solemn care
    'Mongst vulgar thoughts we meet,
        When they possess us with their powers
        Our common self a pigmy cowers.

A fountain of sweet waters is
  Thy look of love. I know
Thy nearness: just as when thy kiss
Tells it with fiery emphasis

And proves our oneness—so
  The tree's rude stock am I, and thou
  The clust'ring, blooming, fruitful bough.

What, doubting yet? Look, where I tread :
  These paths are rough and steep ;
Hope's resting place seems still ahead.
Where are her Eschol grapes? She said
  I'd find them. Yes, in sleep :
    Ay, too, in wakefulness, say I,
    While we remember days gone by.

But I do not despair, for still
  The roughest paths along,
Some flowers crown the bleakest hill :
I hear, as 'twere, some music rill,
  In the morass some song :
    And thou, love, seem'st in all and each,
    Lending enchanting light and speech.

A Canaan full of glory seems
  Today ; while yet thy smile
Around me sheds its love-lit beams :
Tomorrow is a land of dreams ;
  A hope-enchanted isle,
    Where we in peace each other twine
    Beneath our fig tree and our vine.

MY DREAMLAND.

TO MY WIFE.

There's a dreamland I know—I've been in it full
    often :
  The fairies they opened its portals to me ;
And hearts, though as cold as the Arctic, will soften,
  Whenever the smiles of those fairies they see.

I sailed o'er the sea that begirts it with glory,
  Long since, when the summer of boyhood was
    mine ;
And sirens, as sweet as the sirens of story,
  With music seraphic its shores seemed to twine.

No breakers were there where those sirens were sing-
    ing :
  The billows that rolled o'er its sands had no roar :
And the stars, in an odorous azure, were swinging
  Like lamps full of incense the fairy scene o'er.

I saw not a demon of passionate sorrow—
   I met not a spirit of murmuring woe—
I drank not a fountain whose waters were Mara—
   I walked not a path where the buds did not blow.

Meek daisies and violets belted the fountains,
   And streams, with a silver thread, linked all its
      bowers ;
Vine-clad were the slopes of the summer-kissed moun-
      tains—
   The hills wore a chaplet of loveliest flowers.

Though Venus was there in her bowers of myrtle,
   And radiant Adonis in gardens of thyme,
Her voice was the lute of the throat of the turtle :
   And his—it was soft as mellifluous rhyme.

If discord came ever that dreamland to visit,
   'Twas kissed by the air—'twas lulled by the seas—
And melted away into music exquisite :
   Found tongues in the streamlets, and sighs in the
      breeze.

Thus was it long since, when my eyes saw but visions
   Of pleasure and beauty—of love and repose :
And still it is memory's own, and Elysian's
   Soft effluence over it mellowly glows.

The best and the purest—most modest and tender—
  Was given the sceptre, was crowned as the queen
Of the folk of the dreamland—the charm of whose
      splendor,
  By sunlight, and moonlight, and starlight, was seen.

No jewel, bespangled—no garnet or beryl—
  .Encircled the head of this love chosen queen :
No diamond glinted to shame or imperil
  A beauty, whose glory was part of each scene.

Her full orbed enchantment was borrowed from na-
      ture,
  Of all her best glories, her charms was the sum ;
The mold of each limb and the glow of each feature,
  Seemed fresh from the hand of the Good Spirit
      come.

My youth, blessed youth—with a beauty as glorious,
  And eyes that could rival the fairy queen's eyes —
Sailed out o'er that sea with a banner victorious,
  And the gates of that dreamland he took by sur-
      prise.

The queen of the fairies he took as by capture,
  But more like Adonis than conqueror he ;

The pride of his conquest resolved into rapture—
  The captor was captive, a conqueror she.

A home in that dreamland I yearned to inherit,
  When youth took me over that violet sea;
And got in my right, by the gift of the spirit,
  Quit claimed by the queen of the fairies to me.

And I said to myself, " I shall build me—erect me—
  A cottage as simple, yet fine, as can be;
And the folk of that land, they will never suspect me
  Of claiming one pow'r not bestowed upon me.

" This cottage ere long will become a fair villa,
  'Twill grow in the light of the good people's eyes;
And peoples, who come o'er the dark stormy billow,
  Will see it with envy, amazement, surprise."

Now my home was of mountain, and meadow, and
     prairie—
  Well watered of brooklet that laughed through the
     land:
And it looked tow'rd the South, o'er the palace of fairy,
  Whose portals and walls were not builded by hand.

It looked tow'rd the South, over emerald valleys:
  It looked tow'rd the South o'er a violet sea:

And upon it the South wind still emptied her chalice—
  Her spice scented dews from the reefs of the Key.

And nothing but music came up from the willows,
  Where sea maidens sang, by the echoing shores,
Of radiant palaces down in the billows—
  And jewels, all sorts, which besprinkled their floors.

And I said to myself, with a pride unaffected :
  " What's this that the spirit has done unto me?
Who am I, that my virtue should thus be respected?
  I'm earthy as ever the earthy may be.

" My home shall be peopled by none but the lowly :
  None haughty shall enter those portals of mine.
My people shall hate all that's mean and unholy—
  Shall turn them away, lest they sully the shrine.

" But the angels of charity, haply appearing,
  As if to enchantment the portals shall ope ;
For they'll bring to my people sweet messages cheer-
      ing,
  And leave on their faces the transcript of hope."

Now, it ought to be known that we all have our angels,
  That dwell in our bosoms to praise and reprove :
They export and import argosies of evangels,
  And spread them in charms o'er the visage above.

There's mirth and good cheer—there's friendship and
    kindness;
  There's affection and love—they be angels in truth.
There's envy and hatred—two angels of blindness—
  Ingratitude, poisoning his own sugared tooth.

These angels of evil or good on our faces
  Repeat and engrave what they learn in the breast:
And thus are betrayed all the peace-giving graces,
  And thus all the demons that give us unrest.

Come, show me a life that is given to kindness,
  I'll show you a face that is sweet to behold:
And show me another who walks in vice-blindness—
  The night of that life on the visage is scrolled.

So my home, it was peopled by none but the dutiful,
  The light of whose faces the angels kept there;
And many a visitor, splendidly beautiful,
  Found entrance and lodgment its glories to share.

Now, I kept at my gate, in the manner of mortals,
  Good sentries, all comers and goers to see;
And scribes, full of wisdom and truth, at the portals,
  Who, all that got entrance, reported to me.

These told me right oft of a wonderful visitor,
  Well marked for attractions of heart and of head:

Of modest accomplishments none seen exquisiter—
  The gates to whose coming wide open were spread.

The charms of her manner, the grace of her motion,
  The joys of her mouth and the heav'n of her eye,
In the hearts of all dreamland awoke a devotion,
  And quick to her bidding on errands they fly.

They report her politeness as more than politeness,
  It wells like the fountain as grateful and sweet,
And the glow of her face has a soul-kindled brightness
  Which tells us her angels have banished deceit.

They tell me, moreover, she's earthly like others,
  A daughter of Adam and Eve like the rest ;
But beloved and esteemed of all sisters and brothers,
  For virtue and beauty, the modestest—best.

Their simplest description was magic word painting,
  'Twas music and poetry soft intertwined ;
No bombast, high color or gaudiness tainting
  The body of truth they presented the mind.

Alas for her virtue, alas for her merit,
  I said to myself she may come, she may go ;
She's my sorrow I fear, for the gift of the spirit,
  This dreamland on her I can never bestow.

Ne'ertheless, I will search me the valleys and high-
 lands,
 Wherever an excellent woman may be—
The fleece-covered plains, and the fruit-sated islands,
 'Mongst women herself or her copy to see.

For I know if she's mortal and earthy like others—
 A daughter of Adam and Eve like the rest;
In our homes—they're our Edens—our sisters and
 mothers,
 By whom we are troubled—by whom we are blest :—

Our sisters and mothers have chosen and crowned her,
 And set her apart an exemplar to be;
And surely I'll know her when once I have found her—
 As women like her are not many to see.

First I went to the queen of my dreamland, who never
 Aught else but the truth had delivered to me;
She whispered a name made immortal forever
 By him,* who was chained that the rest might be
 free.

---

*Columbus.

——18

Eureka!   How strange!   I've not seen it before;
  The likeness is perfect—the picture is true.
I look to the Highlands, and looking, I know her—
  My love of long years: It is you!   It is you!

LINES TO FRED FERGUSON.

Life is full of sad vexation,
Says each grumbler from his station,
   Captain Freddie,
Looking at the situation
Thro' his "specs" of observation :
And if e'er 'twas true, our nation
Shows it plain on this occasion,
   Captain Freddie ;
In religious aberration,
Economic correlation,
Politics and education,
   Captain Freddie.

We are getting poor and poorer,
And the fact is quite a bore-ah,
   Captain Freddie,
To a man with seven or more-ah,

Crying " rations " at his door-ah ;
And of this I'm doubly sure-ah,
When I fail to pay my score-ah,
                    Captain Freddie,
At the pretty grocery store-ah—
A misfortune to deplore-ah,
                    Captain Freddie.

Somewhat uglier, too, we're getting—
On your " looks," though, I'm still betting,
                    Captain Freddie:
In my case there's no use fretting,
No use sighing and regretting,
O'er this everlasting letting
Down and down, tow'rds life's sun-setting,
                    Captain Freddie,
Yet 'tis some folk's sin besetting,
To be fond of praise and petting,
                    Captain Freddie.

Then, too, as we near the reaper—
Who despises most the weeper,
                    Captain Freddie—
We are getting full of vapor,
Trying, though, to cut a caper,
Like a newsless morning paper,

Which has "nary" man to shape her,
      Captain Freddie:
Till her friends, who can't escape her,
Ere she's dead, in mourning drape her,
      Captain Freddie.

That promotion is not quicker,
I have never been a kicker,
      Captain Freddie;
But I'm waxing sick and sicker,
As convictions come the thicker,
That at virtuous things men snicker,
But in trying moments flicker,
      Captain Freddie;
Who about my failings bicker,
But to get your vote, "let's liquor,
      Captain Freddie.

Rich and poor the wider sever,
In a kind of sulk forever,
      Captain Freddie.
These, who sweat at wheel and lever;
Those, who sit at desks so clever;
These await the smart "receiver,"
Those now sport another "beaver,"
      Captain Freddie;

These despair of more endeavor,
Those poor pity show them—never,
   Captain Freddie.

Some must still keep poor as ever,
Still in debt, not worth a stiver,
   Captain Freddie;
Money running like a river
At their feet, they can't discover,
All they ask is just a sliver
From dame fortune's bursting quiver,
   Captain Freddie;
But alas, they never, never
(Should she smile on me) forgive her,
   Captain Freddie.

Others know not want or hunger,
But they labor long and longer,
   Captain Freddie;
Fortune comes, they see and throng her,
And with chains of brass they thong her;
On the mart they ding and dong her;
In the papers laud and song her,
   Captain Freddie;
Rich and richer, strong and stronger,
So they grow: 'tis then they wrong her,
   Captain Freddie.

And some people love a bother,
Cannot—will not pull together,
        Captain Freddie.
Classes will not trust each other,
Men must tackle one another;
Nothing stronger than a tether
Must unite them; they would rather,
        Captain Freddie,
Take their chances in a pother,
Than to plod on in your leather,
        Captain Freddie.

Some are born to dream of leisure,
With a perfect taste for pleasure,
        Captain Freddie;
Others love to delve for treasure,
'Tis their eidolon, and bless your
Soul, I find them slow to cash, your
Check; they pay it under pressure,
        Captain Freddie;
How they heap it, without measure:
Hide it in some hole or fissure,
        Captain Freddie.

My advice is, you may take it,
Ev'ry act of meanness " rake it,"
        Captain Freddie,

With hot shot, and don't mistake it
For discretion.   Shake it! shake it!
Pledge or faith, oh, never break it:
And your country ne'er forsake it,
Captain Freddie.
You'll agree, then, as I take it,
Life is mostly what we make it,
Captain Freddie.

These remarks are no reflection
On those men who court inspection,
Captain Freddie;
But they strike at—on detection—
Social duty, dereliction,
Which call loudly for correction,
Or our land, section by section,
Captain Freddie,
Will be cursed of each affliction
From its centre—sad prediction—
Outward far in each direction,
Captain Freddie.

Woe to all, then, seeing knowing,
That the tempest cloud is growing,
Captain Freddie;
If they stolid wait its blowing,

Nor awake with purpose glowing
To prevent it—nor stand crowing,
Ere one beam of dawn is flowing,
      Captain Freddie.
None but fools delight in going
Near destruction, or in showing
Courage round the whirlpool rowing,
      Captaia Freddie.

REMINISCENCES

OF A

County Superintendent of Education

REMINISCENCES OF A
County Superintendent of Education

THE SCHOOL BOARD.

PART I.

A rough sketch of the rough machine—
The Board—just as it was, I ween,
> Is important very
> If not necessary
To let you peep behind the scene.

And you may guess, as one by one
I show them, who they are—when done,
> I must assure you,
> They've been brought before you,
Part for instruction—part for fun.

But bear one thing in mind and heart,
Howe'er each looks or acts his part,
    You need not doubt it,
    Nor inquire about it,
One thing is certain—all were smart.

Tho' homelier than home-made sin,
And not put up to charm or win,
    Or to make you jealous,
    No brainier fellows,
E'er helped you up or took you in.

A white-eyed man—raw-boned and tall—
Was number one: hard as a wall;
    Yet in no wise wily,
    Doing nothing slyly,
But open as a summer squall.

He desired school reformation; sought
To accomplish it as he was taught.
    By being steady,
    And being ready,
And honest both in act and thought.

While he made the dodger sweat and squirm,
For the faithful he had still a charm,
    And the modest student,

Plodding and prudent,
Admired and loved him true and warm.

The next was almond-eyed and thin,
Made up of muscle, bone and skin,
    So knit together,
    That which from t'other
No one could tell, until they saw him grin.

A strict constructionist was he—
His pseudonym was scrutiny :
    He seemed forever,
    While being clever,
Trying some flaw or fault to see.

Mathematicians both were these,
And kept the numbskull ill at ease :—
    Stern in their niceness
    And primp preciseness,
The "why" with them was a "disease."

The one was quick—the other slow—
And both were very hard to know :
    Both were non-committal,
    Nor swerved a tittle
By smiles of joy or tears of woe.

The next in order, as in time,
In coming on our Board sublime,
    Scarce came about us,
    Except to flout us,
Or to help some pet of his to climb.

Over our fence into a place,—
When pleasantly he'd state his case,
    And our papers fingering,
    And a short while lingering,
He'd shuffle out with busy pace.

Still in a hurry, bent on trade,
No school talk could his brain invade ;
    It seemed to worry him,
    And from you to hurry him,
If you talked of work that never paid.

The next a teacher—nothing else—
Had vain conceits, and took on spells
    Of proud ambition,
    For high position,
But lacked the force which " place " compels.

He needed friends and money—two
Brave things to have, and got by few :
    So he wasn't mentioned,

Save as good intentioned,
Whose machine some thought had lost a screw.

He kept up with the grammars, as
We keep up with the news—it was
    His boast, that mammas
    Were the best grammars,
Whose lessons schools undid, alas!

The last revised edition made
Confusion more confused, he said :—
    " The boys would jumble it,
    The girls would fumble it,
And teachers try it, for the trade."

Not slow of speech, he lost no chance
To show his thought, sense or no sense,
    The while he wriggled,
    Grimaced and giggled,
His self applause was thus immense.

Yet was he well informed and smart,
And had school methods all by heart;
    And the way to use them,
    And not abuse them ;
So teaching was his certain art.
——19

The next—a handsome fellow—stout
And weighty, in each sense, no doubt,
        With a look half jolly,
        Half melancholy,
And a gait like one inclined to gout.

His clothes seemed gotten up with taste,
But put on, as for taps, in haste:—
        Then he looked so pompous,
        While caterwampus,
His breeches hung about his waist.

He seemed a magnet, as to fun,
Mirth's imps attracting one by one,
        And most Falstaffian
        For cheer and laughing;
So all the bashful boys he won.

Of him whose sketch is just above
The opposite—his strength was love,
        Hating dissension,
        And harsh contention,
He boxed us with a cushioned glove.

In his school studies, at your call,
He made some think he knew it all;
        If he didn't know it

He would never show it :—
Falling on top in every fall.

The next, and last one, on the Board,
Oil on the troubled waters poured :
        When examinations
        Tried the teacher's patience,
And just beyond his limits soared.

He soothed each madam's fond alarm,
For kindness has a mighty charm ;
        If she had assurance,
        He advised endurance,
And managed thus to calm each storm.

The last two sketched, in size and modes,
In ways of thought, were antipodes,
        And checked each other,
        And bore together
With ease, what else were crushing loads.

The fat and lean—the lean and fat—
The light and shadow, and all that,
        In act and nature,
        And in ev'ry creature,
Make sights and forms worth looking at.

So I have sketched the chosen few,
Who heart and head and spirit threw,
    Like consecration,
    Into education,
And to them the people's thanks are due.

PART II.

If you'll be patient I'll rehearse,
Well as I can in simple verse,
    How poor schoolmasters
    Meet sad disasters
Half way, for better or for worse:

Or rather how, all unawares,
We fall into misfortune's snares,
    Whene'er we enter
    The mystic center,
Where toil at each intruder stares;

And justice sits, and half demands
The applicant to lift his hands;
    And rev'rent falter
    Before the altar,
Where uncrowned *skill* a sov'reign stands.

Strange instances I might adduce,
To prove that still a screw is loose
          In man's machinery—
          From smart chicanery
Down to him whom people call a goose.

For little as we think it—when
We know ourselves as other men—
          We, in sore confusion,
          Reach the sad conclusion,
That eight are crazy out of ten.

And, in some way at length, we find
Thro' life we've strictly " gone it blind,"
          No questions asking,
          No reason tasking,
But following fancies sweet and kind ;

Finding the difference, after all,
Between the fool and wise but small,
          Cast in changeful chances,
          Or in people's fancies,
Unless sweet providence forestall.

The wisest by a fateful rule,
At times more foolish than the fool,
          And the strong, no better,

To the weak a debtor;
And the pious fiercer than the ghoul.

The scales are level, as it seems,
And as oft are shaken by our dreams
    (Which come in season)
    As by our reason,
Which, alas, too seldom tilts the beams.

This is a wondrous century
Of push and progress, all agree;
    And 'tis no wonder,
    That some go under,
Shipwrecked on such a stormy sea.

Nor have I been astonished yet,
To see such agony and sweat,
    Where all are pushing,
    And madly rushing,
From fortune's horn a share to get :—

To find some people still ahead;
Others forever begging bread :
    In all conditions,
    In all positions ;
One leading and the other led.

So find we—as it comes to pass—
With ev'ry kind and ev'ry class,
    In education,
    Or occupation,
Old Æsop's lion, fox and ass.

The last one does his level best,
But suffers on the final test:
    But the wily second,
    Tho' a frail one reckoned,
Yielding to pow'r becomes his guest.

Men start together on the tide
Of fortune, sailing side by side,
    With equal chances:
    Each awhile advances,
And for a while with equal pride.

But further on, alack! alack!
One rides upon the other's back:
    One does the "toting,"
    T'other the floating;
One buys the manse—t'other the shack.

One, with some natural taint or sin,
Has an heritage and "blows it in"—
    Like poor wild Esau,

          Playing at see-saw:
Down—up—a mournful "might have been."

One feels or thinks he has enough
To weather seas, however rough,
       Lives fast, gets lazy—
       Loses all, goes crazy—
To the last a braggart and a bluff.

Of ev'ry dozen pushing out
Together on the self same scout,
       One returns to tell us
       Of the other fellows,
Who knew not what they went about.

When moral rot attacks the core
Of all our labors, slow but sure,
       It insidious waxes,
       And their vigor taxes,
Then *results* as *bad luck* we deplore.

Wherefore, I have a tender thought,
Unmixed with censure, pity fraught,
       For fortune squanderers;
       Even tramps and wanderers,
Who, by the times, to crime are brought.

That men are poorly fed and shod
Comes of this moral rot abroad ;
    That boys are vicious,
    Girls meretricious,
Tells tales of their ancestral sod :

Tells of some wicked blood—some taint
That has come thro' sinners—pens ne'er paint :
    Whose woe was merited,
    And has been inherited
By even the innocent—even the saint.

Now teachers, looking after this,
May so build up this edifice
    Of soul and body,
    By prayer and study,
That with God's help, ere long, I wis,

The healthy parts, so strong will grow,
They'll push the dry rot out, and so,
    The soul untainted,
    Like flowers heaven-painted,
Will wear a spotless, heav'nly glow.

And through its channel, as of old,
Before the leprosy took hold
    Of life's Siloa,

With healing power,
Will unsullied roll, as erst it rolled.

Labor, whate'er its class or name,
Accomplished well, is worthy fame,
        And creates an angel,
        As an evangel:
A just reward for us to claim.

So, 'tis not the splendor of the art
That wins for man his little part
        Of reputation,
        Or of honored station,
In shining halls or busy mart:

But 'tis the thing he does, well done,
And by the rule of "three in one,"
        Itself commending,
        By its fair ending,
All things are small beneath the sun.

All things we do, tho' done the best,
Are small beneath the sun, and blest
        Is the brave worker,
        Who is not a shirker,
When duty utters her behest.

Now, when we teach our boys and girls
That Peace her banner still unfurls
          O'er the shrines of duty,
          Not o'er those of beauty,
Nor yet o'er Genius' crown of pearls:

And that thro' Labor's gate alone,
We pass to Honor's lofty throne;
          That by slow percentals,
          Not by accidentals,
In sweat baptized, we win the crown.

Teach them that 'tis man's fate to sigh;
That all complain, and weep, and try—
          Some way or other—
          To escape from bother,
But none succeed, save those who die.

They'll set their faces " tow'rds the hills
Whence comes our help ;" and ills
          Will not much afflict them,
          Halt or deject them,
When grief their cup with Mara fills.

But hope will sit within their hall,
And spread her bright wings over all;
          Banish dejection,

Soften affliction,
Sweeten the wormwood and the gall.

Perchance she'll cheer our mills and looms,
Whose laborers lonely care consumes;
And faith and charity,
That wedded rarity,
Will cheer these almost living tombs.

Joy, too, will haunt our cotton clime—
Our seeding and our harvest time,
And mirth will whistle,
Where thorns now bristle,
And amity will banish crime.

Our shops will be a place of song,
As well as sweat and dreams of wrong;
Our occupation,
Finding recreation,
Swapping labor as we go along.

And, as we know it, careworn toil
Will not be wed to thoughts of spoil,
In ryhme and reason,
In and out of season,
But with rich fruition bless'd will smile.

And, as we know it, galling work
Will not suggest the thought of shirk,
    In rhyme and reason,
    In and out of season ;
Nor will ease at labor sneer and smirk,

When we go teaching duty's claim,
And that in *work* there is no shame,
    But rather glory,
    And food for story,
And material for a princely name.

PART III.

The funny side of folks is seen,
Whene'er we find them tossed between
    Vexations, worries,
    And foolish flurries:
Not while they keep a happy mean.

The *want of money* keeps some folks
Subjects of every joker's jokes :—
    They look so sorry
    When they cannot "borry :"
When they can, they take it as a hoax.

The *want of information* makes
The coolest stumble into " breaks : "
  His grit goes flickering,
  As he feels you're snickering,
And his nerve, when needed most, forsakes.

The *want of confidence*, alas,
Soonest betrays the bashful ass,
  In his role of fooleries,
  And awkward drolleries,
Which a man of common sense ne'er has.

But *the want of self-respect*, of all
The most conduces to our fall :
  At first disarms us,
  And then transforms us,
To something very mean and small.

But when a fellow wants all four,
What a vacuum has he to deplore ?
  What a sad chance has he
  To win his lassie,
Or a decent living, if no more ?

That there are teachers—pardon me—
With all these wants, you'll all agree ;
  Yet they keep on stumbling,

Halting and grumbling,
And why we're laughing, cannot see.

And to make their luck the saddest yet,
They teach from sunrise to sunset,
    Thro' the livelong quarter,
    As they " hadn't ought to,"
And fail a " stiff'kit " then to get.

It's very hard—it's very sad—
And enough to make a Moses mad;
    How much more a sinner,
    Who has lost his dinner,
And feels besides he's treated bad.

I need not add, by way of jest,
That I have sometimes thought it best,
    In this situation,
    Some *information*
Helps the teacher out when sorely pressed.

Then I'd prescribe, just for a change,
To keep his bearings and his range,
    That with *it* well shaken,
    Self-respect be taken,
As an antidote for " big-head mange."

After which, to dull the fevered sense,
Just taken off on *confidence*:
    And then, my honey,
    If you take *money*,
You'll do quite well, at all events.

PART IV.

From out a roadless precinct once,
There came to me a burly dunce;
    A country treasure,
    Beyond all measure,
The most conceited of her sons.

Less fitted than his old grey mule
To electrify a grammar school;
    Though in natural vigor,
    He could cut a figure,
In books and arts he was a fool.

" He was gwine," he said, " to put in reach
Of his ' diggins ' all the parts of speech:
    Spelling and writing,
    And rule reciting:
Yes, all that any man could teach.

" He was likewise gwine to learn the boys
And gals and sich, to stop their noise;
    To obey their teachers,
    And to love their preachers,
And to study loud with all their voice.

" Gwine to show the scollards of his skule,
That jogapher was larnt by rule;
    That hyderstatics,
    And mathew matics,
Just made a man a 'tarnal fool.

" Said the people wanted him, fer why—
'Cause he was for *vox populi*,
    And was always rated,
    'Mongst the eddicated,
Above them ignorant small fry.

" He'd keep the scollards in a run,
Much faster than they'd ever done,
    Or he'd be a blizzard,
    From A to Izzard,
And show 'em he warn't there for fun."

He got his license—"learned " his school,
And was himself the biggest fool,
    Bombastic " play out,"

——20

Of all the " lay out"—
Like cases prove this still the rule.

Another came, a Mister B——,
Whose " Pappy had no use for me,
    Bekase, he hearn it,
    Them as didn't earn it,
Got funds for teaching A B C ;

"And didn't learn the scollards quick,
A poky teacher made him sick :—
    Where gals were foolish,
    And boys got mulish,
He made 'em git thar with a stick.

" His pappy said, ' He paid the tax,
And thought he had a right to ax,
    And know who got it,
    And why, dod rot it,
The Superintenden' hid the facts.' "

These fellows had the confidence,
But the other three they wanted—hence
    Their narrow chances
    To get advances,
From men of dollars and of SENSE.

A Mr. K——, a modest wight,
With brow of most imperious height,
    Looking in upon us,
    And almost won us,
By trembling like the frailest sprite.

I liked the fellow, for his eye
Had something in it, sweet and sly;
    And his voice pathetic,
    Yet energetic,
Convinced me he would do to try.

He had his "blue-black" in his hand,
And came prepared on this to stand;
    For like some others
    Of his haughtier brothers,
He thought the rest a rope of sand—
He thought 't the best book in the land.

" All learning," thought he, " lay behin' it :—
Elocution was a case in p'int,—
    No doubt about it;—
    Schools were lost without it,—
He could teach it, too, up to the j'int."

A Mr. C—— in time applied;
A sister fair clung to his side;

A timid mister,
And a selfish sister,
And both my patience sorely tried.

They'd nudge each other—wink and frown :
She'd whisper—he would write it down ;
He'd take the vapors,
She'd take the papers,
And both got sick and went down town.

A noble rustic made a claim
Upon " them licenses ; " the same
As the nice " two gallus,"
First grade town fellows,
Were paying for, whene'r they came.

He had the money in his " paw, "
To get the best allowed by law,
As for the second,
Or third, he reckoned
He wouldn't plump at them from taw.

On that occasion, you may guess,
He didn't get " them licenses,"
But he kept a-coming ;
And he kept a-humming,
And took a " third grade, " ne'ertheless.

And that persistent man has since,
Upon the sands of time, made prints :
    First he saw his error,
    As in a mirror,
Then yielded to the force of hints.

Little by little on he slid,
By doing well just what he did,
    Strong, energetic,
    With zeal magnetic,
He has never let his lamp be hid.

All sorts and grades of men applied—
The boorish and the dignified,
    The primp, the jealous,
    And the " no 'count " fellows,
The heavy browed—the gentle eyed.

Nor idly did I gaze upon
The crowds that met each month—the fun
    At times was glorious,
    And the mirth uproarious—
For such curious things were said and done.

I could but sit and speculate,
Upon the expression, dress and gait
    Of this and that man,

As our jolly fat man
Summed up each anxious fellow's fate;

And as the mild man of the Board,
As kind and courtly as a lord,
    So sweetly yanked 'em,
    That they almost thanked him,
For being to liberty restored.

I could but watch their features, eyes;
Their make-up—physiognomies—
    And muse and ponder,
    And guess and wonder,
What lay beneath their outer guise.

On one occasion Mr. B——
Kept writing "to be certainty,"
    And Mr. Peter
    Kept saying "creetur,"
Yet both could teach geometry.

And by their side a Mr. M——
Repeated oft, "I taken him"
    To be a preacher,
    And yet this teacher,
In figures caused your head to swim.

It takes all sorts of men to reach
All sorts of people, and to teach
        History and grammar
        To suit one's mamma,
Who learnt in Brown the parts of speech;

And it may be, the neighborhoods—
The rude, untutored solitudes—
        These men demanded
        To mould, rough handed,
The folk according to their moods.

A nice class of men, perchance,
Would have taught the people to advance
        Beyond their neighbors
        And their wonted labors,
And with dragon's teeth thus sowed their haunts.

'Tis best by slow degrees to rise—
We get to floundering otherwise;
        Ere we 'tempt the ocean
        In its wild commotion,
Let's try the wave which placid lies.

From enterprise to enterprise,
By natural stages, go the wise;
        When with leap or gallop

The folk develop,
They snap their wonted bonds and ties.

To teach geography to one,
And reading to another son,
        And speech reciting
        And ev'n hand writing—
A pretty art when neatly done—

'Tis the teacher, not the book, that's sought,
The man and not the science taught:
        Not the lesson hearer,
        But the message bearer,
Where characters are to be wrought.

As sparkling as we ever see,
But rather rusty was Miss P——,
        And she had a father
        That thought her rather
The smartest thing that came to B——.

So Miss would raise a mild complaint—
Sweet as she was, she was no saint—
        When examinations
        Caused her perturbations,
And then her pa, he put on paint.

They fretted—then we fretted—then
The angry Miss, she bit her pen,
    And sulked and pouted,
    And we half doubted
She'd ever look so sweet again.

"Can't furnish brain," said I, "I'm sure—
Can ask you questions by the score."
    Then answered pappy,
    Half fierce—half happy—
"In course, you hain't no brains to spore."

He said it with a whisper, yet
So clear and sharp it came, it set
    The house to giggling,
    And me to riggling;
And Miss got o'er her pouting pet.

Take in the picture of the Board:
The white-eyed, heartless man encored,
    The lean man "follered,"
    The fat man hollered,
And pap kept with the crowd and roared.

The superintendent tried to frown,
Awhile looked up, around and down;
    Then pap, confound him,

Winked at all around him,
And hurried out down to the town.

It was indeed a solid shot,
And enough to bring me to the thought,
      That oversmartness
      Well-merits tartness,
To whip it till to sense 'tis brought.

A genial teacher, and a wight
Jealous of each and ev'ry right,
      Was Mr. Moses;
      And counting noses,
He thought he'd give the Board a fright.

Qouth he, "Our disposition he saw,
Teachers would call us now to taw;
      And he was ready
      And willing," said he,
" To put it to the test of law.

" First we'll make the superintendent show
His law for doing thus and so:
      By what authority,
      Our small minority
Large majorities could overthrow:

" We'll claim our ' stiffkits ' for the pay."
And then he frowned and looked our way,
    And our collar tightened,
    And we got frightened,
And hemmed—but knew not what to say.

He saw he had us on the scare,
Tip-toed—put on a tragic air—
    And glaring ghastly,
    Declaimed his lastly,
And stalked, ere " busting," to his chair.

We, the ugly Board, bewildered sat,
Till one defendant raised his hat,
    And half suggested,
    And half requested :
" If he might ask who'd bell the cat ? "

Hearing a titter, with a grin,
He took the situation in ;
    It seemed to strike him,
    And the others, like him,
That the " fuss and feather " talks don't win.

" 'Tis well," we said, " to watch the rat—
And from him draw this lesson : that
    The loudest chiding

Are the first ones hiding
When called upon to bell the cat."

Well, teachers are like other men,
And have their grievance now and then ;
    Somewhere or other
    They find a pother,
Which breaks out on or tongue or pen ;

And, being flesh and blood, they do
What gets them oft into a stew ;
    And what with dickering
    With fools, and bickering,
They borrow troubles not a few.

Now, once upon a time, we had
A case before us that was sad
    And also funny ;
    For at bottom money,
More than morals made the people mad.

One able, jolly pedagogue
At times came up to town agog,
    And in his leisure,
    Would have no pleasure,
Unless 'twas bottled in a jug,

We had him up for getting down,
And putting on our sternest frown—
    And our frown was awful,
    Almost unlawful—
And shadowed him from heel to crown :

But with the pluck of artful clown,
He seemed to relish this our frown ;
    So with language candid,
    We reprimanded
Him for smiling all the way from town;

Of course, he owned up like a man,
Was ready for our bar and ban ;
    But the prosecutors,
    Who were fierce disputers,
Must talk, and so the talk began.

A—— said he was a drunkard vile
(In his own pocket all the while
    Was hid a bottle
    To wet his throttle).
B—— swore he was too mean to " spile."

K—— cotch him lying, as he swore,
Right 'gin the tree at the church door.
    R——, him defying,

Said as for lying
That never 'stonished him no more.

He knowed that B—— and A—— and K——
Were lying—drunk or sober—day
And night, and cheating
As much at meeting
As any whar, so it would pay.

So grew the pow-wow hot and loud,
Till reason left : the angry crowd
In that situation,
Righteous indignation,
Was like a fire-fly in a cloud.

To stop the arguments, blood red,
One of the judges rose and said :
"Let's dismiss the sinner
And go to dinner—
That man that never lied is dead."

The plaintiffs, one by one retired,
Nor of our verdict e'er inquired ;
They only wanted,
As they loudly vaunted,
To see that this, our pet, was "fired."

Close on the heels of this strange case,
A lady told us to our face,
        In terms inelegant,
        We wern't intelligent—
Of course we thought this out of place.

But I've digressed, and have forgot
To mention others in the lot,
        Whom to think of dazzles,
        And tears to frazzles
Our reason like a solid shot.

The women—bless the women, all—
The homely, handsome, large and small ;
        Those wondrous creatures,
        By nature teachers—
They gave me, with the rest, a call.

Some curious women tho' have come
To take a little license home ;
        As for book-knowledge,
        Got at school or college,
That was a little bothersome.

Yet some had sheepskins, some had none,
But as to fitness—'twas all one,
        With just this difference,

I gave the preference
To sheep skins, as I should have done.

One thought her license came too high,
But paid it with a little sigh ;
    Another thought it
    Cheap, so she got it—
She knew 'twould pay her by and by.

One girl, all of a sudden—quick
As she got seated well—got sick
    In contemplation
    Of examination,
Which after all she thought a trick.

Another, ere she spoke a word,
Captured the fat man of the Board,
    And made the lean one
    Grin like a green one ;
And for ev'ry smile a ten she scored.

She was not beautiful or smart,
But she had a magic art
    In look and action,
    To our satisfaction ;
For with her heart she touched the heart ;

And rightly felt the Board, and thought
She was by art and nature brought
    To school room duty,
    Wherein soul—beauty—
Does more than mind has e'er yet wrought.

Such fitted her to be a guide,
A kind of angel on this side
    The stormy waters,
    To lead our daughters
And sons across the dang'rous tide.

Another scene to glance upon,
A few more touches, and I'm done:
    There is yet another,
    The friend and brother,
Who sought "them licenses and fun."

The picture's most imperfect, till
We paint poor Cuffy at the mill,
    His turn awaiting
    To get pro-rating,
Just enough for seed corn in the hill.

But ne'ertheless he always came
On time to register his name—
    When there was money—
——21

His face all sunny ;
And right or wrong he had a claim.

His way of getting up a school,
Tho' conflicting with the legal rule,
        Or as right directed,
        Was to be expected,
And showed him far more knave than fool.

Ev'ry negro woman, man and child
In his township, on his list he filed,
        As material proper
        For his school hopper ;
And for all he drew on me and smiled.

One Cuffy, smarter than the best
Taught thirteen months a year, and guessed
        The time remaining
        He would spend in training,
For a fifteen months' heat after rest.

Well, all in all, the nation's ward
Out of the " kinks " is pulling hard ;
        And for straightout swearing,
        He is past comparing,
For he swallows oaths as Laps do lard.

Trials of ev'ry kind had we,
Yet side by side in unity
    We've slowly crept up,
    And bravely kept up,
With the commissary train, you see.

And when our hist'ry's truly writ,
  Not what we've taught will brighten it ;
    But our way of standing
    And respect commanding,
When disaster conquered all but grit.

A SCHOOL ROOM FIFTY YEARS AGO.

There's nothing in the realm of thought,
    Of hidden things and dark,
Men have not from its hiding brought:
    They've struck some shining spark,
Out of each myst'ry, in these fruitful years,
And used it for smiles or bodeful tears.

The bowels of the crusty earth,
    Rock-ribbed, have yielded fair
And monstrous things, and given birth
    To wonders past compare;
And out of darkness streams of light have flowed,
Which, tipped with chemic sticks, have blazing glowed.

The unseen elements of air,
    Caught by man's wary hand,
And by his science unaware
    Bound, waiting his command,
Are now our message-bearers—both of woe
And pleasure, war and peace—and flying go.

They weary not of man's strong spell—
    Led by the weakest hand,
Themselves the strongest Ariels,
    Instant they belt the land,
The stormiest sea ; instant they come and go
Bound to the thought that leads them to and fro.

The catalogue of wonders wrought—
    Itself a wonder—talks
Like fiction—seems with fairy fraught.
    But daily in our walks
We see what doomed to Bedlam ancient seers,
For talking of them, ere these fifty years.

And 'tis most fit with curious eye,
    Into the vaults of years
Long dead and buried, now to pry
    With reverential fears,
And ask responses from these oracles,
Touching the hist'ry of our immortelles.

To tell of the youth of those rare men—
    Those heroes, poets, sages,
Inventors—who with sword and pen
    Have made our history's pages
Read like Arabian Tales—tell whence they rose,
How they were reared—their childhood's joys and
    woes.

And chiefly in what classic walls,
    Their early years they passed;
Whether in art or science halls,
    Their glorious lot was cast;
Or out among the hills in cabin rude,
They got their inspiration's homely food.

Did they by gilded mansions go,
    O'er paved or graveled way?
And through the city's sinks of woe,
    Plod schoolward day by day?
Or thro' the happy fields—thro' sylvan bowers,
Around them rocks and streams and birds and flowers.

Did they go moping on their course,
    Half stupid, half forlorn?
To their fair fountain; driven by force;
    Clouded their life's sweet morn?
Or went they vigorous, glad, with joy, to taste
The fountain bubbling sweet out in the waste?

Let History answer from the vaults
    Of dead and buried years,
Where wondering Admiration halts
    And their responses hears.
'Mongst the rude hills our heroes, statesmen grew:
There life's best lesson learned full well, though few.

Our Fulton, Morse, and Edison;
    Our Stonewall Jackson true;
  Forrest and Pelham, Beck and Brown,
    Douglass and Lincoln, too:
Garfield and Yancy—and as great as they,
In other times, our Webster, Jackson, Clay.

  All spent life's early morn remote
    From gaudy school and shrine;
  Each on the rock of Fortune smote
    With spell— wand-like, divine—
And to their hardy smiting, whence 'twas stored,
The fountain of success in affluence poured.

  Their lessons in this solemn life
    Were conned in cabins low;
  Familiar from their birth with strife,
    It lost for them its woe:
The log school house a paradise appeared;
And all through life its glories they revered.

  What sweet instruction may we draw,
    From noble lives like these?—
  Lives that enchant us, while they awe;
    Make us tremble while they please:—
What lessons from their deathless histories
Which gild the vaults of buried years? 'Tis this:

He, who would walk on heights sublime,
    Or lead or guide the van,
Or dare the ladder higher to climb,
    Must be a *hardy* man :
And, to sustain himself in that high bourne,
His hardy lesson at the foot must learn.

Suffice it, we will think of days
    That have been, when these men,
Now shining lights along our ways,
    Made sport in glade and glen,
Or peeped out at the play-grounds, thro' the cracks
Of the log school house, where they got their whacks.

In those days all the boys got whacks :—
    And even the girls, at times
In their soft palms, on their dear backs,
    For those sweet smiling crimes
Of snickering low across the house at us,
Got "hail, Columbia," or "e pluribus."

Well, 'twas a glory—in that past
    Of fifty years "lang syne,"
When wealth, not yet in towns amassed,
    Spread out its wings benign
O'er all the land, o'er hill and mead and plain,
In fleecy fields, or fields of golden grain.

It was a glory then to view
    The cabin on the hill :
The rude log cabin, old or new,
    Beside the crystal rill ;
And ere the dew had left the balmy air,
To see the country's young folks gathering there.

Mayhap, in lowly rill-lulled vale,
    The humble structure rose
A kind of Mecca, where the flail
    Dispensed, till daylight's close,
Prophetic hints of future usefulness,
To each disciple it proposed to bless.

There lone and lonesome long it stood,
    Yet known both far and wide,
" This Mecca of the mind " so rude,
    The simple people's pride ;
Ay, more ; the pride of good folks far away—
" The Doctor got his larning here," they say.

" And that big lawyer down to town,
    He graduated here :
Thar 'twas that great man Joseph Brown
    Stayed, Jo did, two whole year :
He was a cur'us fellow—lor's a mussy—
He'd beat an all-fired cane-brake bein' fussy.

 “ You never yet have saw such men,
    As got their larning thar :
My Julius larned to use the pen,
    When taught by Jack O’Bar ;
He larned to cipher, too, at any sum :
And thar he kissed Sal Grubbs—he did, by gum.

 “ You never seed sich boys and gals,
    They got plum thro’ ; they said
The elements—the *wills* and *shalls*—
    And kept ’em in thar head :
They studied loud, and sounded like a blizzard ;
And *Alfred Betty* got from A to Izzard.

 “ The pa’son, too—a shining light
    In all the worl’. Tom Duff—
Got most of all his larnin’ right
    Under that school-house ruff :
Tom got it thar ; I knowed him mighty well,
He sot a heap, one time, by my gal Belle.”

That rude log hall of learning stood
    With gaping eaves and sides,
Yet near it the sounding wood
    Were classic walks and rides ;
And many a puncheon seat, whereon the boys
Worked out their “ sums ” and spelled with earnest
    noise.

Within the house, with look severe
    Or gentle all by chance,
The pale school master sat, the seer
    Of those charmed classic haunts.
And with a kind of back and forward sight,
Saw all in front, behind, to left and right.

    " Git quiet thar, you boys—
        Thought girls were always fussy,
    And kept the whole house in a noise ;
        But you boys—lors ha' mussy—
I never knowed a set so mean and lazy ;
The rumpus that you make will run me crazy.

    " Tom Childress, watch them feet of yours,
        And keep 'em off of Lou's,
    I saw you winking out o' doors,
        And making signs at Suse.
Thar, Lou ! that look, I think is mighty sassy ;
What are you comin' to ?   Oh, lors ! ha' massy."

    And all day long, above the hum,
        The good man's voice was heard ;
    Now flew the hick'ry cross the room,
        With scarce an angry word:
A moment—and the whacking echoed round,
Attended with full many a squirm and bound.

Tho' rude and most unclassical
    The language of these teachers,
On them let not the censure fall,
    But on the social features
Of the broad land in which they nurtured grew,
And the companionship of youth they knew.

We get our *language*, while we stray,
    About our home with nurse;
Her talk and sayings ever stay
    A blessing or a curse:
The deepest graven in the mind and heart,
And science vainly bids them go: depart!

No mottoes hung above his door,
    Some moral sense to teach;
But through the cracks and crannies pour
    What deeper lessons preach:
The glaring sunshine and the pelting shower,
Speaking of heaven's and stormy nature's power.

The lessons which they teach are deep
    And broad, and widening still;
And wake the spirit from its sleep,
    And the whole being thrill;
And those, who understand them, wisdom learn
Broader than that poured from the classic urn.

The autumn's rain and winter's sleet
  Swept thro' it like a wave;
Yet the huge log fire, with generous heat,
  A warm reception gave.
And Boreas, coming chill our knucks to freeze,
Transmuted grew a friendly zephyr breeze.

Here boys are taught that lesson, best
  In each vicissitude,
Proud self-reliance : not to rest
  Secure on purse or blood,
But, with eyes front and forward step, to sweep
Obstruction back, or o'er it conquering leap.

The soft and soft'ning influence
  Of artificial charms,
And pleasing helps and comforts—hence,
  Insidious noxious harms
To man's well-being—never here were found,
Nor with their purse-bought chains their victims bound.

Nay, nay—the sky, the air, the earth,
  In calm or storm ; the tree
In bloom or fruit; the varied mirth
  Of wind-harp or of bee ;
The echo-waking stream ; the wild rose-bower :—
These were the sources of mind, spirit-power.

No desks well ordered, all in line,
　　In that rude shelter stood ;
No folding seats that polished shine,
　　(But seats of rough-hewn wood),
To lazy comfort lured the girl or boy,
And took from study what it gave to joy.

　　Rude seats and rough are fit for those
　　　Who scorn the soft'ning arts ;
　　Who deal with power, sledge-hammer blows,
　　　Be they on minds or hearts ;
Despising sick refinements, sickening ways,
While yet with all its noble parts ablaze.

　　Now, other things than mottoes, maps
　　　And benches make a school :
　　These are the ornamental scraps,
　　　Which polish up a fool :
To character (the building up of which
Is the aim of teaching) they don't add a stitch.

　　The teacher is the school: indeed,
　　　The teacher must be found
　　Ahead of those, whom he would lead ;
　　　Or standing on a round
Above those whom he'd teach to climb the ladder :
Those whom he'd give light to, he must overshadow.

To be all things to all, appears
  The teacher's highest art :
To tickle cross-grained Mr. Sneers :
  To humbug Mrs. Smart :
To walk a chalk line, when the Goodies frown,
And know just when to knock young Upstart down ;

To walk among this varied crowd,
  And harmonize with all ;
With some to joke and laugh aloud,
  With some to kneel and crawl :
With some to whisper low, with words precise :
With some to speak imperious, with advice ;

To laugh always when Mr. Fun
  Tells his side-splitting jokes—
Tho' they've grown ancient 'neath the sun
  And dry as mummied folks—
To sigh when Mr. Grumble sighs, and feel
His mis'ry from your cranium to your heel;

And chief of all, to use the books
  Which papa used at school ;
And wedge 'em in my hooks and crooks
  Like any other fool ;
Uncle and auntie, too, must have their " say,"
And if you would succeed you must obey ?

To talk this way and that, to meet
    Emergencies and squeezes:
To *every* gale to spread your sheet:
    Then when by blows and breezes
You reach your post, tho' torn and tempest-wracked,
For heaven's sake call the boat you rode in, " *Tact.*"

Ah, there were giants in those days,
    Rough, strong from Nature's hand!
Calhoun and Bentons, Websters and Clays,
    Each in himself a brand
Plucked from the altars of the free, to fly
With meteoric light athwart our sky.

They learned their ugly A B C's
    Upon a puncheon seat,
And manly stood the biting breeze,
    And calmly bore the heat:
They looked to *Him*, who taught them, for the lore
They needed--not to wall or desk or floor.

And there were angels in those days:—
    And ne'er a wing had they:—
Young women, full of matchless grace;
    Now old, care-worn and gray—
The household gods, for whom we've built our shrines,
To whom Experience still the palm resigns.

Tho' stricken now by years and woe,
    And wrinkled, worn and gray;
The soul that lit them long ago,
    Still lights those eyes today;
For still the chaplet which then twined the brow—
The chaplet of rare virtues—twines it now.

The olden fire and vigor glow
    Behind the withered cheek;
And gentle smiles and graces show
    Far more than words can speak,
And noble courtesies and deeds so charm,
We half forget the change of face and form.

We do not mark the sunken eye,
    Nor find repulsion there:
We give the tribute of a sigh,
    Yet own it bright and fair;
In shattered forms we see what Heaven gives,
The deathless beauty of true stainless lives.

Were ever rosier girls than they,
    The queens of broad domains?
And never city belle could say
    She wove more jeweled chains
Round nobler, braver, stouter hearts than she,
Who bowed bofore this country dominie;
——22

For there beside the window sat
    The rich man's daughter, Nell;
And in yon corner was that brat,
    Who led us all by her spell.
And near her, just behind the door, was Hattie,
And my Matilda Jane—we called her "Mattie."

If in the far, thin-settled hills,
    This bower of learning rose :
What strange, what sweet remembrance fills
    Each scene around, and glows
Within the heart, with an enchanting spell,
And makes the tenderest emotions swell.

The wandering evangelist
    Here poured his fiery plea,
And bid the anxious sinner list,
    Siloa's pool of thee ;
Here told *His* woes, whose simplest word or will
Made water wine, or raging storms be still.

Here told of Isaac's race and power—
    A moral pointing, too ;—
And led his hearers hour by hour
    With Hagar, sad and true,
To the parched land—from Abram doomed to fly,
To where she laid her Ishmael down to die.

Here charmed the list'ning throng with tale
　　Of Jacob, wily seer :
Of Esau wild, whose matchless wail
　　Wakes even a stoic's tear :—
" Bless me, too, oh, my father ! "—such his cry—
" Thy erring, wretched Esau, ere thou die."

He spoke of Penuel's altar, where
　　The human and divine,
In marvelous wrestle strove (despair
　　And hope in giant twine) ;
All for a blessing—then the startled crowd,
With mingled sighs and tears in silence bowed.

Here Joseph's woes and triumphs told :
　　Here Israel's wanderings long :
Here of the great law-giver, old
　　And weary, from the throng ·
On Nebo's height, in Moab's land apart,
Canaan in sight, dying of broken heart :

Of Ruth, who lay at Boaz's feet :
　　Of Samuel : " Here am I : "
Of David, Zion's psalmist sweet,
　　Anointed from on High :
Of Absalom, who fell ere yet his time was ripe :
Of Jonathan, true Honor's prototype.

So there's a halo round these piles,
    These structures rude and plain :
For the halo of sweet memories smile ﹔
    As the Pleiads o'er the main,
Or like the faithful Cynosure, whose light
O'er unknown billows guides the bark aright.

    These mem'ries sweet around us glow,
        No matter where we roam,
    And still a mellow radiance throw,
        Like that which crowns our home;
And looking back upon the old play-ground
Her sister *Home* still by her side is found.

    Ere long upon these old play-grounds,
        The old school house will fall,
    And be but crumbling, mouldering mounds,
        Unmarked at length by all.
To mem'ry only known : and where they stand
Structures will rise the marvel of the land.

    Or plow-boys, plowing o'er the mounds,
        Will mark with curious eye
    The strange debris about the grounds,
        And then go whistling by :
And hags will tell the boys and girls, perchance,
Some fearful tales of them and call them haunts.

Yet, when they've gone, they'll leave their mark
    And their messages behind :
And men may read them in the dark,
    Those treasures of the mind,
And they'll show golden increase—not dead leaves—
When the angel comes to gather in the sheaves.

POEMS

OF

MEDITATION.

POEMS OF MEDITATION

THAT HUMBLEST PRAYER.

" Dear Lord, all good, make others great,
But keep me innocent."

The moonlight slept upon the wold,
  The curfew's voice was still,
And fitfully the tinkling fold
  Wake new echoes on the hill:
A soft hand, that of Scotia's queen,
  Honored the window pane,
As with her star-eyed diamond pin
  She traced what should remain
On heart, as well as glass and plate,
  This rarest sentiment:
Dear Lord, all good, make others great,
  But keep me innocent.

Resounding vault or echoing aisles
    Where song or prayer awake,
And friends with their approving smiles
    Say, brother, sin forsake:
Fair sisters plead and mothers lead,
    And fathers gone before,
All make us feel a fitful zeal
    To seek the other shore.

Aroused and stricken, lo! we pray,
    Our better spirit stirs;
Yet from the goal we're far away,
    Till the poor heart breaks like hers:
Till like the Queen in low estate,
    All our soul on heaven bent,
Dear Lord, we cry, make others great,
    But keep us innocent.

I've had the sin-clouds in my day
    To settle o'er my heart,
And where they touched, and where they lay,
    They curdled ev'ry part.
Like swampland's blist'ring, poison dew,
    Sweet scented, cool and bright,
The more their charm, alas, for you!
    The more their fatal blight.

So now, I pray with the sweet Queen,
  The sweetest prayer of all
(For those who walk with spirit clean
  Care not when shadows fall),
Sweet prayer for high and low degree,
  Like inspiration sent,
Dear Lord, all good, make others great,
  But keep me innocent.

We pray for health—for earthly goods—
  For freedom from our woes,
And often in our higher moods
  The tear in anguish flows.
We sigh, we rave, with varied plea,
  Thinking His ear to reach:
Some standing, some on bended knee,
  With wild or formal speech:
But when we pray the humblest prayer,
  Forgetting self the while,
Asking of earth's best things no share,
  But only heaven's smile:
These words express the holiest state,
Like an inspiration sent:
Dear Lord, all good, make others great,
  But keep me innocent.

CONSECRATION.

Are you waiting, woeful brother,
    In the starlight of this shore,
For the helping of another
    When this solemn night is o'er?
You will ponder—you will wonder—
    In a multiplied regret,
Vainly wonder—vainly ponder—
    Till the last faint star is set.

Are you hoping, troubled brother,
    In this hurly-burly pit?
You may hitch on to another
    Who shall drag you out of it:
You will hope on—you will grope on—
    Dark and darker to the last,
Vainly grope on—vainly hope on—
    Till escaping time be past.

In ourselves the strength is lying,
    Joy to win or woe to bear;
And the test of strength is trying,
    Not in hoping 'gainst despair.

Consecration—abnegation—
  Knocks the horror out of strife :
Abnegation—consecration—
  Glorify the humblest life.

Be yourself a fagot blazing,
  Be yourself a flame of light :
Then the rav'n her black wings raising
  From your realm will take her flight.
Raven haunted—woe enchanted—
  For awhile your bark may be :
Woe enchanted—raven haunted—
  'Ne'ertheless you'll cross the sea.

Ev'ry soul 's a spark of heaven
  Glowing in its mould of clay ;
By the darkness it is driven
  To desire—to seek the day.
Ever jealous—ever zealous—
  So it grows and spreads and springs,
Ever zealous—ever jealous—
  Till it wins its royal wings.

What a glory then surrounds us,
  In our very pains and woes ;
Scarce the cloud ahead confounds us,
  Ere resolve some light bestows.

In the life time of a strife time,
  Good men oft are torn and riven :
In the strife time of a life time,
  Good men are prepared for Heaven.

Are you weary, suff'ring brother,
  Sick and sore from hope deferred,
Full of sorrow altogether—
  Poor, unpitied, and unheard ?
Mighty heroes, Cæsars, Pharoahs—
  At their fortunes make complaint :
Cæsars, Pharoahs, mighty heroes—
  Sceptred, crowned—are sick and faint.

Princes, fresh from vic'try winning,
  Oft'ner than the yeomen faint,
Clothed in purple and fine linen
  Bow before the ragged saint.
That much higher—that much nigher—
  To the lightning freighted air :
That much nigher—that much higher—
  To the precincts of despair.

MY SAVIOR, NEAR TO THEE.

How sweet when tempests cease,
  And soft winds take the sea,
To feel that grateful soul of peace,
  Which draws me near to Thee :
  My Savior, near to Thee.
    And through my lifted eyes,
    Up joyous towards the skies,
      My thoughts to pour,
  Glad as the bird set free—
  Glad as the ship at sea—
  When those dark tempests flee,
    And terror 's o'er.

How sweet when Winter flies,
  To greet the coming Spring ;
To turn to Thee our smiles, not sighs,
  To weep not, but to sing
Our praises, Lord, to Thee.

To gaze on Spring's gay mood,
And feel our joy renewed,
    Our hope—our song—
Sweet as the verdure's growth,
Sweet as the genial South,
Warm kisses in her mouth
    The whole day long.

PRAYER.

ONE STEP ENOUGH FOR ME.

I would not wail nor even make complaint
      At circumstance,
I still would hope, nor pine, nor sigh, nor faint,
      Could I advance
My prayer: to get a little nearer Thee—
Day after day—One step enough for me.

On ev'ry hand the darkness gathers thick,
      And I'm afraid:
My soul is weak and my remembrance quick,
      My hope near dead;
In mercy then consider, pity, see,
And help me on—One step enough for me.

Unlovely have I been, so fatal long
      In error's thrall,
That habit holds me easy with grip strong;
      I stumbling fall
So readily, unless I'm propped by Thee,
Lend me Thy hand—One step enough for me.

——23

Let me advance; no light remaineth here,
            I've tried this scene,
And found not yet one place of sacred cheer,
            Of living green :
From all I've known as yet I can but flee :
Help me press on—One step enough for me.

Dispel the deep'ning darkness : show the light—
            The life—the way :
Forgive in me the bitter past, the night
            Of sorrow stay.
Help me press on, a little nearer Thee ;
Day after day—One step enough for me.

THE ESCHOL LAND.

Thou hast been with us, when flying
    Egypt's bondage to be free,
And our olden selves denying :
    Through the depths we followed Thee.

Thou has been our Guide when fleeing
    O'er the waste towards Horeb's brow,
Ev'n to Moab—Canaan seeing—
    Do not let us falter now.

Drink and manna sweet affording,
    Thou hast led us by the hand;
Help us now across the Jordan,
    To fruition's Eschol land.

COME, BROTHER.

Come, brother, and go with me over,
    I'll give you a berth in my bark;
By the light which she bears you'll discover
    The billows when stormy and dark :
            Fear not—fear not—
Jesus is walking the wave.

Come, brother, and go over yonder,
    I'll lend you my staff and my rod,
Through the gloomiest gloom I can wander,
    For my light is the smile of our God.
            Fear not—fear not—
Jesus has promised to save.

Come, brother, I'm crossing the valley
    Of the shadow of death ev'ry day;
Remember we never must dally,
    You are lost if you stop by the way.
            Fear not—fear not—
Jesus is there as your guide.

Come, brother, through darkness and sorrow,
  Through danger—through all but despair—
He'll cheer you from morrow to morrow,
  And crown you with rest over there.
          Fear not—fear not—
Jesus with us will abide.

Come, brother, wherever I guide you
  The Savior has promised to be,
And whatever misfortunes betide you,
  You'll forget them when heaven you see.
          Fear not—fear not—
Jesus will surely repay.

Come, brother, my pleading 's now ended,
  My bark is now ready to sail,
Beware of a Savior offended,
  'Gainst God can no mortal prevail.
          Come now—come now—
Jesus says, come on to-day.

HYMN OF PRAISE.

Lord, of the mighty land and sea,
I hear thy word where'er I be,
Thou speakest through each sense of ours
Thy boundless sov'reignty and powers.

I gaze upon the bloomy tree,
And catch some beauty glimpse of Thee;
I watch the lulling waterfall,
Its silv'ry lips to worship call.

The dark, lone mountains far away
Suggest thy temples ev'ry day,
The mighty, rolling river shakes
The soul, and mention of Thee makes.

The floating clouds—the tideless breeze—
The rolling orbs—the frothing seas—
The wing of day transparent white,
The mystic, star-bespangled night:

All speak a dumb, prophetic lore,
And for us sweet instruction pour
A new song put into our mouth,
From East and West—from North and South.

THANKSGIVING.

Lord of the harvest hear us, lo,
After long toils—'tis sad, 'tis so,
Gathering our crop, we find our sheaves
Mostly composed of thorns and leaves.

Only a few tares did we sow—
None that we ever dreamed would grow,
But in the soil of sin's dark breast,
Somehow the tares have thrived the best.

How we repent us it is so,
Lord of the harvest, mercy show ;
Poor, like ourselves, our gift is, take
What we now bring for mercy's sake.

Cause but the little we lay by
Under thy smiles to fructify,
Then will the thorns and tares, no doubt,
Be wholly crowded, smothered out.

Lord of the harvest, hear our prayers,
And help us trample out the tares :
Smile on the soil of sin's dark breast,
And then the wheat will thrive the best.

COMMUNION HYMN.

Savior, while at this typic shrine
  We bend the suppliant knee,
Oh, let thy smile about us shine,
  And charm our thoughts to Thee.

Let not these thoughts distracted pause,
  While from this sphere they flee,
But, as the sun the vapor draws,
  Attract them, Lord, to Thee.

Or like pent streams, which meeting go
  Resistless to the sea,
In one great river let them flow
  To their great Ocean—Thee.

GOD'S OMNIPRESENCE.

Lord, I see Thee round me ever:
  On the ocean, on the land,
In the darkly rolling river,
  In the sunshine on the strand:
In the wild moan of the mountain,
  In the silence of the plain,
In the prattling of the fountain,
  In the waving of the grain.

In the voices of the wildwood,
  Of merry birds and busy bees,
Where a kind of endless childhood
  Fresh'ning holds the sward and trees;
In the gladness of the shower,
  Born of sullen storm and cloud,
In the birth of winter's flower
  Leaping from its snowy shroud.

In the summer garden's pleasure,
  In the winter woodland's woe,
That in bloom of boundless measure
  This enrobed in spotless snow.

In each white eyed Atacama,
    Turned to glass when heaven smit,
In the snow land of the Llama
    By red Cotapaxi lit.

In the rivers of the ocean,
    In the islands of the sea,
In the tempests wild commotion,
    Lord, my fancy painteth Thee:
On the hill tops—in the valleys—
    When the peaceful zephyrs blow,
When the festive South wind dallies,
    Where the North winds howling go.

Lord, thy woodlands tell the story
    How thy handiwork excels,
And a faint glimpse of the glory
    Cometh whence the fountain wells:
In each sand encircled Fezzan,
    Beautiful and bright and blest,
Land of fruit and balmy resin,
    Land of water, peace and rest.

All around and all above us,
    Having language true and sweet,
Things which tempt and sorely prove us
    Point the footprints of Thy feet.

Yet thy footsteps in all places
    Still by day and night we see,
And my glance some beauty traces
    Which were vanished but for Thee.

In the pathways inward leading
    Towards thy temple's shining door,
In the church bell's loud mouthed pleading
    To the peoples, rich and poor.
In their sighing at thy altar,
    Bowing head or bending knee,
In the hymnal or the psalter,
    Intimations come of Thee.

In all voices, utterances,
    In all forms and faces, Lord,
In our day time, night time, trances—
    In the Felt, the Seen, the Heard :
In the night queen's light so tender,
    In the starlit upper sea,
In the sun's most boundless splendor,
    Glimpses come and proofs of Thee.

THERE'S A TIME FOR ALL THINGS.

There's a time for all things, surely,
  As the good old saying goes;
But the time for labor sweating,
And the time for money getting,
  An unbroken record shows.

There's a time they say for laughing,
  And a time as well for song:
But the time for circumspection,
And for honest heart conviction,
  Seems to be the whole life long.

There's a time some think for dancing,
  Others deem it rash and vile:
There's a time for being merry,
But the time for being cheery—
  Cheer is comely all the while.

There's a time for being dressy,
  Glossy as a new made dime,
Picture like in its completeness :

But the time for person neatness—
  That's demanded all the time.

There's a time, no doubt, for weeping,
  Be they penitential tears:
But the time for meditation
On the promised reservation—
  That should haunt us through our years.

There's a time for public worship:
  Heaven—aye earth—this much requires;
But to worship Truth and Beauty,
Nor to tire of doing duty,
  Should be food for all our fires.

There's a time for pray'r in public:
  Peace on earth, good will to men
This suggests; but private prayer
Claims its time in joy or care,
  And all nature breathes, "amen."

There's a time for all things godly,
  Things in harmony with right:
But the time for doing evil,
Or compounding with the devil,
  Is but honored in its flight.

BE THOU WITH ME.

When in youth and manly vigor
  My path I tread,
And a wreath of shining blessings
  Entwines my head ;
Keep my heart from proud presumption,
  Vain glory free,
And lest in self I trust me,
  Be Thou with me.

Should I gather wealth or treasure
  By varied scheme,
And of power and dominion
  I haughtily dream :
Then the source of these my blessings,
  Let my eyes see,
And lest even then I mind not,
  Be Thou with me.

Should I reach the height where Honor
  Sits down with Fame,

And the horns of reputation
    Blow me acclaim :
In that pivot of temptation
    To forget Thee,
That I may keep my balance,
    Be Thou with me.

But if in sore misfortune
    I bow me down,
And in each coming prospect
    I see a frown :
My sword, my staff and buckler,
    My solace be,
And in my desolation,
    Be Thou with me.

So be I rich or needy,
    In joy or pain ;
So be I weak or mighty,
    In loss or gain :
In the ups and downs of changes
    My Shepherd be,
My Comforter and Savior,
    Be Thou with me.

BEATING AGAINST THE BARS.

The boundary line is fixed, and yet
  On daring wing we rise,
And soar and soar, and all forget
  The unknown beyond us lies.
In vain we search the deep
  Past sun and moon and stars,
Thus far, no-farther go,
  Beating against the bars.

Ah, we may struggle and rebel
  'Gainst warning, fact and sign,
But the unknown and unknowable
  Are just across the line.
In vain, alas, in vain
  We are vaulting tow'rds the stars—
In vain, alas, in vain
  We go beating 'gainst the bars.

The best and worst of us alike
  Are in an iron cage,
And in our agonies we strike

The sides with fruitless rage :
Alas, alas, in vain
    We are vaulting tow'rds the stars—
In vain, alas, alas,
    We're beating 'gainst the bars.

Thus far, no farther, the decree
    Our limit fixed declares :
Thus far, no farther, woe is me,
    Can I ascend the stairs.
In vain the sigh, the tear,
    The moaning tow'rds the stars :
In vain our bruised hearts
    Are beating 'gainst the bars.

WHERE JESUS TROD.

Lord of the changes, heed our pleading,
  Out of the struggle bring the lull :
A plenteous crop from faithful seeding.
  To workers true a garner full.

Lord of the folk of toil aweary,
  Lord of the hearts by sorrow bowed,
Soften their fortunes hard and dreary,
  And be their cries of need allowed.

Lord of the valley and the mountain,
  Whose homes with incense burn for Thee,
Let altars rise at every fountain,
  And crosses guard each stormy sea :

Peace, like a dove, perched on those crosses
  Calm to the billows dark will bring,
And 'round those altars hope's green mosses,
  By living waters kissed, will cling.

Spread over all faith's mantle golden,
  Down from the city of our God,
And contrite, broken hearts embolden
  By faith to tread where Jesus trod.

OH, LAND OF LANDS BEYOND THE SEA.

Oh, land of lands beyond the sea,
  Where dwells the peerless King,
Ev'n to this shore there comes to me
  Scents of thy endless spring.

The odors of our fading flowers
  Are like Elysium blown,
What then be those which glad thy bowers,
  Land of the Great Unknown.

Low lolling by some silvery stream,
  We talk of balmy rest,
And touched by Love's sweet nymphs we dream
  Of being sometimes blest.

Fair, flitting fancy, like the mist
  'Round the red face of dawn,
When her gold hair dew besprent is kissed
  By the flood light of the sun.

”Tis most enchanting, lovely, whiles
  O’er hill and vale it plays,
And for long hours of gloom, with smiles
  And odorous breath, it pays.

But swift it rises, melts, is gone,
  So flit our fancies fair ;
Not so the joys that meet that dawn
  Which bathes them over There.

WHEN I LIFT UP MY EYES.

When I lift up my eyes, and lo,
  The darkness closes round.
I ask me which way can I go
  While darker doubts confound:
What, what is left me but to stand
And cry: Lord take me by the hand.

No matter what the darkness then,
  Within me or without,
My sweet bird over and again,
  Hov'ring my path about,
Keeps whisp'ring me in faith to stand
And cry: Lord, take me by the hand.

So through the Shadow's Valley way,
  Whilst passing down to cross
The River, where the Light is, may
  That faith my thoughts engross,
And make me feel—aye, understand—
That Christ is there to take my hand.

I doubt not, then, 'mid the gloom,
  The deepest that may brood,
If such a *grace* my spirit plume,
  But that my attitude
Will please the Master of the land,
Who'll come and take me by the hand:

To lead me onward, and beyond
  The dismal scenes of death,
Unconscious that a more than wand
  Of magic is true faith,
Which both the people and the land
Transmutes when we take hold His hand.

I AM IN THY PRESENCE.

I am in Thy presence : and I know,
  Though gloom be round me cast,
Thy hand will lead where I should go,
  If I but hold it fast.

I am in Thy presence : every day
  As up my path I roam,
Some scene persuades me that my way
  Is towards another home.

I am in Thy presence : and I trust
  As flesh the weaker grows,
The noble spirit in its dust
  The warmer vigor shows.

COME, THOU HOLY SPIRIT.

Come, Thou Holy Spirit, rest
  Daily—nightly—in my breast,
Hold this erring will of mine
  Fettered close and strong to Thine.
Day by day—day by day—
  I go erring from Thy way:
Holy Spirit, bide with me
  Till I learn to cling to Thee.

Come, Thou Holy Spirit, break
  Satan's chains for Jesus' sake.
And the darkness of my way
  Light with Thy unclouded ray.
Hour by hour—hour by hour—
  Clouds of sorrow round me lower:
Holy Spirit, bide with me
  Till I learn to cling to Thee.

AT THE BEAUTIFUL GATE.

When our wanderings cease at the beautiful gate,
  And weary and almost despairing we wait
For the angel to take off our burden of sin,
  And opening the portals, to bid us come in :
How sad will it be, if the burden has grown ;
  Such a part of ourselves, that he'll leave it alone :
And as sin never enters the beautiful gate,
  Oh, how long, oh how long, we must wait, we must
      wait
        In unending sadness,
         If not madness.

Dear brother, dear sister, the burden today
  May be washed by one drop of the Fountain away ;
In the realm of the Spirit sin's curse is not known,
  'Tis here but a part of the flesh and the bone :
Unwoven its tendrils with those of the heart,
  And now it is easy to tear them apart—
This done, when you come to the beautiful gate,
  But a moment the angel will cause you to wait :
      Not in grief—not in sadness—
        But in gladness.

IMMORTALITY.

'Tis a helpful thought to cherish,
  When life's fiery trance is o'er,
And these cunning hands shall perish,
  And these eyes shall shine no more:—
That this substance with a story,
  Never voiced by human lips,
Shall shine on in changeless glory,
  When all else is in eclipse.

'Tis a helpful thought, when sorrow,
  Like a vulture, eats the heart,
To reflect, that on the morrow.
  Like a shadow, 'twill depart;
That it has but eat the rotten
  And the canker, after all,
And the sap which fed them gotten:
  Thereby breaking its own thrall.

THY STILL, SMALL VOICE.

Oh, that to me, thy wayward child,
  The upward way were clear,
That when enticements sweet beguiled
  Thy still small voice I'd hear,
And like a little child obey,
    Nor go astray.

That with these earth-dimmed eyes of mine,
  A glimpse I might but get
Of that Elysium where the vine
  And fig tree flourish yet,
And olive green begems the shore
    Forevermore.

And glad with hope, like singing bird,
  Which tow'rds the day dawn springs,
I'd hear the music of Thy Word,
  And press tow'rds better things;
I'd glimpse the glory of thy shore
    And hope once more.

Now tow'rds the empyrean I go forth
   To soar and sing elate,
But bound by what I am to earth,
   To earth I gravitate:
I flutter down on feeble wing
      And wail, not sing.

Oh, Jesus, Savior, thou canst break
   This sin's magnetic force,
And from my hands the shackles shake
   And from my will the curse:
And from my mind, my spirit's sight,
      Dispel the night.

And spite of sin's inherent power,
   From its bondage set me free,
When 'neath my vine and fig tree bower,
   I'd rest and worship Thee,
And sing thy mercy, glory, praise,
      Through all my days.

HOW SWEET THEIR CLOSING YEARS.

How sweet their closing years
　　Whose feet have ever trod,
While in this vale of smiles and tears,
　　The paths that lead to God.
The paths which lead to God,
Which all the prophets trod
　　　With bleeding feet,
Yet with a purpose true:
Heaven's battlements in view,
Angels their journey through
　　　To meet and greet.

When pleasure's smiles allure
　　We can but go astray,
But following virtue's compass sure
　　We'll find at last the way.
We'll find at last the way,
Which in the olden day
　　　Elijah trod:

And spite of bitter woes,
And spite of madding throes,
Can but be trod by those
    Who seek their God.

So may this life of mine
  Thro' all its joys and woes.
Like yonder cloudless sun decline,
  In peace its journey close.
In peace its journey close,
Outside this land of woes ;
    Where the star of even—
Whose lamp enchanting guides
Faith's followers o'er the tides
And o'er their past abides—
    Is the eye of Heaven.

I'LL BE THY CHILD.

Though I were strong to lead my people forth,
  Like Moses, through the desert lone and wild:
To give the law to princes of the earth
  And wear the potent sceptre at my girth,
And feel I stood to Thee unreconciled:
  I rather were content, methinks, to lay
My sceptre down, and lose my power to sway,
          And be Thy child.

Though I might claim as mine the mystic key
  To unlock the door where Croesus' wealth is piled:
Though haughtier rulers suppliant come to me
  And at my portal envious bent the knee,
And fame's rare crown this fitful life beguiled:
  If this should close Thy door on me, it were
But transient joy—much, much would I prefer
          To be Thy child.

FATHER, STILL GUIDE ME.

Joy may bring smiling
With its beguiling,
Peace make the spirit haughty and brave,
But on some morrow,
Smitten by sorrow,
What from despair that spirit can save.

Time, the stern smiter,
Is a requiter;
Grief comes to wound us, time brings the salve;
But if, when stricken,
Faith does not quicken,
Time turns to rot the healing we have.

I have been gladdened
Often as saddened,
I have been cured as sickness befell;
Still go I straying,
Passion obeying,
Still 'gainst myself and Heaven rebel.

Father of kindness,
Healer of blindness,
Take not Thy Holy Spirit from me,
Keep Thou beside me,
Father-like guide me,
Draw me, tho' stumbling, nearer to Thee.

FROM A MYRIAD LEAFY LYRES.

Thy mercy like the stream, oh, Lord,
  Flows gladding all its banks,
Let me like tree and plant and bird,
  Return perpetual thanks.

By morn and eve the flowers exhale
  Their od'rous lives away,
And grateful birds in grateful vale
  Pour their ecstatic lay.

The wind with freight of dew outspreads
  Her tireless, cheering wings,
On hill and vale the warm wave sheds,
  And grass to meet it springs.

To parching lands a coolness bears,
  And tempers thus their fires,
And ev'ry twig its joy declares
  From a myriad leafy lyres.

BLEST REDEEMER.

Savior in this dread Sahara,
  Where the sands are deep and hot.
And the water streams are Mara,
  Parching, weary : leave us not,
      Blest Redeemer :
What are we of Thee forgot?

Near the haven still we ponder,
  Happy Canaan just in sight,
Through the burning sands we wander
  Sad and sadder day and night;
      Blest Redeemer,
On our pathway shed Thy light.

Here we walk in gloom and shadows,
  While from Horeb we behold,
Over Jordan's happy meadows,
  Waving vineyards, fields of gold;
      Blest Redeemer,
Guide us to those joys untold.

STRONGER THAN THE HILLS.

Leave, ah leave me not alone,
　Prayer of prayers for all to pray;
Whether sitting on the throne,
　Whether in the straw we lay,
Weary, labor stricken—leave,
　Leave us not alone to grieve.

Leave, ah leave me not alone,
　In the struggle or the strife,
To allurements that are strewn
　In the path of ev'ry life;
All my strength is gone from me
　When I am not stayed by Thee.

Leave, ah leave not alone:
　What is man, without Thy aid?
Like a puppet overthrown
　By the storms himself hath made;
Strong with Thee, without Thee weak,
　I must still Thy comfort seek.

Leave, ah leave me not alone,
    Weakest of created things,
When Thy comfort is withdrawn,
    And Thy hand no helping brings:
Stronger than the hills, the sea,
    When we stand or walk with Thee.

PEACE WILL YET BE MINE.

Lord, whatever cares there be
  In each coming hour for me,
And they fall like night to day,
  Making very dark my way:
If thy smiles about me shine,
  Peace, sweet peace, will yet be mine.

So the burdens that I bear
  Shall not crush me to despair,
But the more the nerve they strain
  And stress the soul and rack the brain,
That much less shall be the soul's
  Yearning after earthly goals.

Nor shall sorrow I now see,
  Bodeful threat'ning unto me,
Make my spirit sore afraid,
  If the hand which Moses led
Through the sea, the waste, the foe,
  Half that mercy to me show.

MAKE OUR POOR HEARTS WHOLLY THINE.

Lord, the contrite heart and broken,
    Saith the bard, thou'lt not despise :
Speak again as Thou hast spoken
    Peace to those who agonize.
Speak to me—speak to mine—
Mercy on us, we are Thine.

What Thou gavest Thou has taken,
    And as mortals we're bereft,
And as mortals feel forsaken,
    Spare the portion Thou hast left:
Low we bend--I and mine—
Whole or broken, we are Thine.

Thou hast told us, not a sparrow
    Falleth but Thou heedest it:
Tip with pity, then, the arrow
    Which our heart of hearts has smit:
Pity us, me and mine,
Smit to dust, for we are Thine.

We believe Thou never blightest,
    'Tis not Thine to wound or harm ;
Thou wouldest rather, what Thou smitest
    Into higher types transform.
So transform me and mine,
Make our poor hearts wholly Thine.

TESTIMONIAL POEM FOR THE KNIGHTS OF PYTHIAS.

It is well when the leaves of the forest expand,
  And the blossoms grow sweet in the glen,
And the voice of the turtle is heard in the land,
  And the vines spread their tendrils again,
And the spring throws her mantle of joy at our feet,
And with varied enchantment invites us to meet,
That we gather as brothers each other to cheer,
And to point out the glories that round us appear;
And to think just awhile of the brothers we've known,
Whose sweeter enchantments are vanished and gone;
And to cast on their graves just one poor fading
    flower,
And thus honor their ashes one sad, passing hour.

It is well like the leaves of the forest so green,
  That verdant our memories should be,
And sweet as the flowers which garland the scene,
  From bramble to blossoming tree;

And to keep all these memories still verdant and
    sweet,
At the door of the Lodge their shades we should greet,
And fondly recall all the deeds they have done.
And fondly recount all their victories won ;
And learn there a lesson of wisdom perchance,
By mortals learned only in such sacred haunts—
For never such light by the living is shed,
As comes from the fires of the beautiful dead.

Not long will these roses their beauty retain,
    They will fade ere tomorrow is gone;
But the stem whence we pluck them will blossom
    again
    In response to the kiss of the dawn.
And a lovelier crown than we've culled will it show,
Ere the sands in the glass of tomorrow run low,
And the beautiful tints, that now vanish and fade
To the mystic alembic in which they were made,
Will return and be mingled again o'er and o'er,
And come back to charm us and vanish once more :
Some new transformation presenting each day,
And some new enchantment to brighten our way.

Thus the fancies now uttered, the praises now sung,
    May fade like the leaf of the rose,

But the fountain of memory, from which they have
    sprung,
  Still lovingly, constantly flows :
Still utters its tender complaint and its sighs,
And soft as the voice of an echo it dies,
O'er the loved ones and lost, that are ours nevermore.
Yet the oftener you stir it, the deeper t'will pour :
And methinks while we stir it today, and return
To the days when their fires, like our own, used to
    burn,
Speaks a voice, while a halo around us is shed :
Next to love for the living is care for the dead.

Men are things of the past, in their hopes and their
    fears,
  In their wise and their foolish desires,
Which are watered as t'were by the tide of its tears,
  And warmed by its smouldering fires.
'Mongst the past's hoary ruins and mouldering tombs,
The loveliest flowers of our coronet blooms,
And the present is blest and the future made bright,
By the charms which remembrance keeps bringing to
    light;
While the deeds of our brothers, long silent, long
    dead,
Around us a halo all beautiful shed.

Thus today's tree of life has its root in the past,
  And the branches—the leaves and the fruit—
Are debtors in part, in their vigor and cast,
  To the vigor and soil of that root.
And the dead are not really dead, as it seems,
But they walk in a land like the land of our dreams—
They hover about us on memory's wings.
Ah! the beautiful dead tell us beautiful things,
As they linger around us all lovingly yet,
And when we forget them, ourselves we forget.

'Tis for such that we gather in solemn parade,
  With reverent rites, to proclaim
The remembrance of pledges and vows we have made
  In friendship and charity's name.
For the love that we boast of is nothing in truth
If it serves but to tickle the fancy of youth ;
If it breathes not the oracles, comfort and peace,
To Damon and Pythias seeking release
From chains of the tyrant or fetters of woe—
If it fails in this work, 'tis a poor mimic show.

So we'll scatter the roses nor care if they fade,
  Whlle the stem whence they came does not die ;
And we'll sing all our praises, tho' swift to the shade
  Of oblivion's realms they should fly ;

While the fountain of memory rolls deep day by day,
I will furnish new stories when these pass away.

Yet we come to the graves of these brothers of ours,
    Not to wail in the ears of the dead;
Nor to fear, tho' the shadow thus over them lowers
    Nor a mantle above them to spread :
But to freshen our thoughts of the living who stand,
Heart broken and weary—no staff in their hand.

To freshen our thoughts of the orphan in need ;
    To strengthen our purpose and vow ;
To bind up the wounds of the hearts that now bleed,
    And the widow's just claims to allow :
'Tis for this, more than all, in the cold and the heat,
Round these graves—round our altars--we gather, we
        meet.

What we do for each other in glory and shame,
    As we worry and struggle along,
Lends a spirit of beauty and grace to our aim.
    And inspires like a magical song :
Some poor, worn out brother, who faints in defeat,
And pines more for friendship than clothing or meat.

So we'll gather again and again to renew
    Some ties that are breaking or broke ;

To call down a blessing on Gentile and Jew,
    As bearing one burden—one yoke ;
And out of our oracles, bitter and sweet,
We will learn what is proper, and do what is meet.